"My mind is a complete blank," Robin said, her eyes tearing.

"It will come back to you in time," Jake said. Hoped.

"I get the impression I don't have time."

Jake shoved his hands into his leather jacket pockets.

"Someone's after me, aren't they?" she said in a soft voice.

"You're safe here in the hospital."

"You're kidding, right? I almost died in the E.R., then a crazy cop handcuffs me and accuses me of being involved."

Jake took a step closer. "It won't happen again. I'm here and I'll make sure no one gets to you."

"I'm afraid of what comes next," she said.

"Don't be. Just rest. That's the best thing you can do for yourself."

She nodded and closed her eyes and he suddenly wondered if this was his chance at redemption. He'd see Robin through to the end and make sure she wasn't another innocent victim of violence.

Books by Hope White

Love Inspired Suspense

Hidden in Shadows
Witness on the Run

HOPE WHITE

An eternal optimist, Hope was born and raised in the Midwest. She began spinning tales of intrigue and adventure when she was in grade school, and wrote her first book when she was eleven—a thriller that ended with a mysterious phone call the reader never heard!

She and her college sweetheart have been married for thirty years and are blessed with two wonderful sons, two feisty cats and a bossy border collie.

When not dreaming up inspirational tales, Hope enjoys hiking, sipping tea with friends and going to the movies. She loves to hear from readers: hopewhitebooks@gmail.com.

HOPE WHITE

Witness on the Run

Love Inspired

Recycling programs
for this product may
not exist in your area.

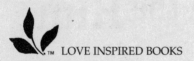 ™ LOVE INSPIRED BOOKS

ISBN-13: 978-0-373-44443-4

WITNESS ON THE RUN

www.LoveInspiredBooks.com

Printed in U.S.A.

Be strong and take heart,
all you who hope in the Lord.
—*Psalms* 31:24

To Larry, for your amazing support, encouragement and love.

ONE

Monday couldn't come fast enough for Robin Strand.

As she packed her briefcase with the printouts of checklists and sign-up sheets for tomorrow's pediatric cancer walkathon, she took a deep breath and reminded herself she loved her job as a special events coordinator. And she really did, but sometimes having alternate hours than the rest of the world was a drag.

On cue, her cell rang. She eyed the caller ID. *Jenn.*

"Hey, Jenn, what's up?" Robin said.

"We're waiting for you at the Five Spot."

"What time is it?" She swung her briefcase over her shoulder and flicked off the desk lamp.

"Nearly nine."

"I don't know, Jenn. I've got so much work to do before the walkathon Sunday."

"You're not at work, are you?" she scolded.

"Uh…"

"You *so* shouldn't be there, Robin. Come on, swing by the Five Spot. Right now. I'm ordering you a longhorn burger as we speak," Jenn said.

Robin's mouth watered. "You're cruel, you know that?" She locked up the office and headed to the elevators. Being a part-time receptionist, Jenn didn't have the same level of commitment that Robin had for her work.

"You really need to come join us," Jenn added. "I got us a two-for-one deal on dinner."

Robin noticed light streaming through an office down the hall. She thought she was the only one dumb enough, or most lacking a social life, to be at the office on a Friday night. Then again the building was home to its share of overachievers like Destiny Software Design, Remmington Imports and Vashon Financial.

Then there was Robin, whose job was her life. Since she was in charge of Sunday's walkathon for the Anna Marsh Pediatric Cancer Foundation, she would probably be back here tomorrow working on volunteer rosters and donation lists.

"Hey, Trevor just showed up," Jenn announced.

"Great. My hair's a mess, my make-up is nonexistent, and I'm exhausted."

"Tough. Get your fanny down here."

"Thanks, but..." Her voice trailed off as movement caught the corner of her eye. Robin glanced into the Remmington Imports office on her right.

And froze at the sight of a tall, bald man aiming a gun at a second man who slowly raised his hands. Shocked and unable to process what she was seeing, Robin couldn't move.

A resounding *bang* made her shriek. Every cell in her body screamed *run!* But for half a second her legs were paralyzed.

"What was that?" Jenn's voice cried through the phone.

Robin stared through the window at the limp body on the floor. Blood spread across his crisp white shirt and seeped into the carpeting.

"He shot him." Then her gaze drifted up from the wounded man to the shooter.

Cold, black eyes stared back at her. Death eyes.

He stepped toward Robin, pointed his gun...

She took off like the eighth-grade, track-and-field champ that she once was. *Do it for your brother. Make him proud.*

Her brother, Kyle. Looks like she'd be joining him soon.

In heaven.

"No," she groaned, turning a corner. She had more to do. She wasn't ready to leave. She had to raise money for children's cancer research. And, she wanted to raise a few kids herself someday.

Swiping her card, she ducked into the break room, flipped the lights off and crouched low to keep out of sight. She'd hide in here and call the police. Her phone, where was it?

The door beeped, and her heart jumped into her throat. The shooter had a passkey? She dropped to the floor, crawling through the darkened break room away from the killer.

Killer. She'd just seen a man murdered. In cold blood.

"No use running," a male voice called out.

Robin took a slow deep breath and continued her crawl toward the exit. *Think! Pull the fire alarm.* That would bring help. But they wouldn't show up fast enough to save Robin from this monster.

"I like the dark, too," he taunted.

In the window's reflection she spied the guy pointing his gun under tables, ready to pop off another round.

Into her.

She whipped open the door at the other end of the room, lunged into the hallway and pulled the fire alarm. Water sprayed from the ceiling as she scrambled to the stairs and hurled herself toward the ground level.

Pfft!

A bullet ricocheted off the wall mere inches from her head. *Focus, girl!*

"Get back here!" the man called. "A witness is on her way down. North stairs," he said in a calm voice. "Take her out."

Hoping to throw him off, Robin flew down three flights, whipped open the door and raced to the south stairwell. She couldn't die tonight. There were a thousand people depending on her to run the cancer walk Sunday.

Strange, the odd things that rush through your brain when you're being chased by a killer.

She practically tumbled down the last two flights of stairs to the street level and threw open the door. Now that she was outside, she couldn't get to her car in the basement garage.

"Hey!" a tall, broad-shouldered man called, crossing the street.

"Take her out," the killer had ordered.

She spun around and sprinted in the opposite direction, braced for the bullet that would surely hit her square in the back.

But he didn't shoot her. She sensed he chased her, but she was fast, fueled by adrenaline.

For Kyle, Robin had said, as she'd placed her medal on her brother's trophy. His one trophy. He hadn't had time to win more.

"Stop!" the man called out.

Closer. He sounded too close.

She glanced over her shoulder—

A car horn snapped her attention to an SUV careening toward her, brakes screeching. Before she could react, it hit her, slamming her to the pavement and knocking the wind out of her lungs. As she struggled to breathe, all she could think about was how disappointed Mom would be. After all, it was Robin's job to make her parents doubly proud in order to ease the pain of losing a child.

Robin glanced up at the dark sky, hoping her brother would be the one to take her to heaven. Suddenly, her view was blocked by a man's blue-green, intense eyes.

"Don't move," he said. "Everything will be okay."

She closed her eyes, and a tear trailed down her cheek. *I'm coming, Kyle, I'm coming.*

Jake Walters paced the emergency room like a man waiting on the birth of his first child—only the woman he worried about was a complete stranger.

He couldn't shake the terrified look he'd seen in her eyes.

Or the look of surrender before she'd closed them.

He'd thought for sure she was dead, killed running away from him and into the path of a moving vehicle.

But he'd meant her no harm. He'd been on a stakeout for his cop buddy Ethan Beck when he'd seen the petite woman flee the building as if she'd just seen a ghost.

Or a murder.

Minutes after the ambulance arrived at the scene, Ethan, a detective with the Seattle P.D., had called Jake to let him know a report of shots fired at the Chambers Building had been called in by a cleaning crew, and Ethan was on his way with backup.

Jake had told Ethan about the woman fleeing the building, and Ethan had asked Jake to stay with her until the ambulance arrived. Yeah, like anything could have ripped Jake away from the woman's side? He'd felt responsible for her condition.

Now, an hour later at the hospital, Jake paced the E.R. waiting area and fisted his hand. The brunette was a stranger, and Jake had no legitimate reason to be here, but he'd stay close until he knew she was okay.

He leaned against the wall next to the E.R. doors and waited. He'd done his share of waiting with Mom as she'd fought the cancer that had taken her life.

Waiting drove him nuts.

"Jake?" Ethan said, walking toward him. Two of his men trailed close behind. "Hey, man, thanks for hanging around."

They shook hands. Ethan and Jake had grown up together, fought off bullies in their Seattle neighborhood together, and joined the army together. Although they'd been split up in Iraq, they'd reconnected after they'd shipped home and had ended up in similar fields: Ethan, a detective for the Seattle P.D., and Jake, a Homeland Security agent, recently turned private investigator.

"How is she?" Ethan asked.

"They're not telling me anything. I'm not family."

Realization colored Ethan's eyes. "I'm sorry. I shouldn't have asked you to hang around a hospital. Go on. Take off."

"I'd rather stay, thanks. I feel responsible for this woman."

"Yeah?"

"She was running from me when she got hit."

Ethan eyed him. "Was she running from you or someone else?"

"She tore out of the building like it was on fire."

"I'll bet she witnessed it," Ethan said, his voice low. "Detective Cole Edwards was shot and killed tonight."

"Man, I'm sorry."

"Did she say anything, give you any indication she saw what happened?" Ethan pressed.

"She whispered a name—*Kyle,* I think—then fell unconscious."

"Thanks, buddy." Ethan slapped Jake's shoulder. "I'll take it from here."

"I don't think she's in any shape to talk to you."

"Oh, she'll talk."

Ethan nodded to his men to stay in the hall and pushed open the E.R. door.

"E," Jake called after him, but Ethan had disappeared. Jake didn't like that Ethan might plan to pressure a fragile woman.

Robin Strand. Jake had looked at her ID in her wallet so he'd be able to give the hospital a name to go with that adorable face. There, he'd admitted it. The woman was adorable with her round face and subtle freckles dotting her nose. He glanced at the E.R. door. He hoped Ethan was being gentle with her, but considering a cop had been murdered, Jake wouldn't be surprised if Ethan had a hard time being sensitive to her condition.

"You're Beck's army buddy?" asked a tall cop with a crew cut. He had a scar running across his right eyebrow.

"Actually, we've been friends since grade school."

"Long time."

"Yep."

"I'm Detective Henry Monroe." They shook hands. "This is Gabe Dunn."

Gabe nodded and shook hands with Jake.

"You were with Homeland Security?" Monroe asked.

"Yep. Took a leave of absence and decided to go into business on my own."

"How's that working out?"

"Long hours, but it pays the bills."

"Your connection to the girl?" He nodded toward the examining area.

"Don't know her. ID says Robin Strand. Lives in Seattle, Greenlake, I think. I'm guessing she works in the Chambers Tower. She had a building pass."

Detective Monroe pulled out a small notebook. "What were you doing at the Chambers Building?"

"Stakeout for a client."

Jake suspected that Ethan hadn't told his men that he had enlisted Jake's help. Ethan had called last week asking if Jake had time to keep an eye on the after-hours activity at the Chambers Building, keep track of who came and went and at what times. Ethan knew something was going on in that building after hours, he just didn't know what.

"What client?" Monroe asked.

"Confidential." Jake wasn't giving that up until E gave him permission to do so. When he'd called Jake, he'd said he suspected some kind of police corruption and needed to keep Jake's involvement on the q.t.

Monroe narrowed his eyes at Jake. "Uh-huh. What time did you see her leave the building?"

"At 9:07."

"Was she alone?"

"Yes."

"And she was running?"

"She was. I got out of the car and called out to her. That

freaked her out even more, and she took off down Seneca. She didn't get more than a block when the SUV nailed her."

"We've got officers at the scene questioning the driver."

"It wasn't his fault."

"Perhaps, but there's a good chance Ms. Strand witnessed the shooting of Detective Edwards and needed to be silenced."

"Was Edwards working a case?"

"That's confidential."

"Where did you find the body?" Jake asked.

"I'm supposed to be asking the questions," Monroe said.

The E.R. doors swung open and Ethan marched out, worry lines creasing his forehead.

"Well?" Detective Monroe asked.

"She doesn't remember anything."

"About the shooting?" Jake asked.

Ethan pinned him with angry eyes. "Anything. As in, she can't remember her name, where she's from, what day it is."

"That's convenient," Detective Monroe said, snapping his notebook shut.

Jake eyed the detective. "Convenient?"

"Sure, if she's involved."

Not in a million years, Jake thought. Fragile Robin Strand was no more a criminal than Jake was good father material.

"Doctor is calling it traumatic amnesia due to the blow to her head," Ethan explained. "It's temporary."

"How temporary?" Monroe pushed.

"They don't know," Ethan said. "We all want this guy, Monroe. We're just going to have to be patient or find him another way."

"If the perp thinks she's a witness and doesn't know about this amnesia thing, then she's still in danger," Jake said.

"Then she should remember quick so we can put the guy away," Detective Monroe snapped.

"It's not like she's choosing to forget," Jake said.

"No?" Monroe challenged.

Ethan stepped between Jake and Detective Monroe. "Dunn, you stay and watch over Ms. Strand. Monroe and I will get with the crime scene investigator."

Detective Monroe didn't move at first. He stared at the E.R. doors.

It was devastating to lose a brother in blue and frustrating to know the eyewitness was unable to help.

Or unwilling?

"Thanks, buddy," Ethan said, shaking Jake's hand again. "You've done more than enough."

"Hey, E, I need to—"

"Later, okay?" He started down the hall with Monroe, turned and said, "Go home, Jake. Get some sleep."

"Hey, I don't take orders from you anymore," Jake said in reference to their childhood roles. Ethan had played an army major and Jake a sergeant. Even then, they'd dreamed of serving their country.

Ethan waved him off and disappeared outside.

Jake glanced at Detective Dunn, who stood rigidly beside the E.R. doors pressing buttons on his cell phone. Dunn was tall, husky and angry-looking. Sure he was. A brother had just been killed, possibly a friend. Jake had lost his share of those in Iraq.

"How long have you been a cop?" Jake asked.

"Ten years," Dunn said, not looking up.

"Before that?"

"Military."

"Yeah. Me, too. Which branch?"

The E.R. doors burst open and a young nurse glanced at Jake, then Detective Dunn. "Who came in with Miss Strand?"

"That would be me," Jake said. "Jake Walters."

"She's asking for you."

Detective Dunn raised a brow.

Jake shrugged and followed the nurse. Dunn shadowed Jake—a bit too close, in Jake's opinion.

The nurse hesitated beside a curtain and turned to Jake. "We had a hard time calming her down and didn't want to oversedate her because of the head injury, so please don't upset her."

"Yes, ma'am."

The nurse slid the curtain open. "Robin? This is Detective Dunn and Jake, the man who brought you in."

Robin slowly opened her eyes.

"I'm Detective Dunn." Dunn identified himself.

"You wanted to see me?" Jake said.

She looked at Jake and furrowed her eyebrows as if she struggled to focus. Then she frowned. "You. You were in the street. When I was… I was running.…" Her breathing quickened and she looked like she was going to hyperventilate.

The nurse eyed the blood pressure monitor. "It's okay, Robin." She motioned to Jake. "Please leave."

He hesitated, not sure what had just happened or how to fix it. "Sure. Okay." Then he shot Robin a comforting smile. "I'll be right outside."

She looked away, the nurse hovered over her, and Jake walked out, running an anxious hand through his hair. What had just happened?

He'd frightened her; that's what.

A burn started low and spread through his gut. Jake's memories surged to the surface. Her terrified expression looked way too familiar.

It reminded Jake of what he feared most. Becoming his old man.

Robin might have drawn a blank on ninety-nine percent of her life, but for some reason Jake Walters had spiked panic in her chest.

Being chased, threatened.

She knew the man named Jake, wearing a leather jacket and a silver chain that peeked out from beneath a black, V-neck

T-shirt, hadn't threatened her. She'd never forget the sparkle of those amazing blue-green eyes as he'd leaned over her.

Everything will be okay.

Her panic eased remembering the sound of his voice.

She'd been running for her life. She knew that much. But who had she been running from, and why had Jake been there?

A sudden bang made her grip the sheets to her chest with white-knuckled fingers. She'd heard that sound before. Twice.

Red filled her vision. Oozing across the floor. Blood?

"Robin?"

Robin glanced at the nurse.

"Someone dropped a tray. That's all," the nurse said.

Robin nodded. She remembered her name. That was a good sign, right? Or had someone told her Robin was her name? *Rats.*

"You're safe now," the nurse said.

Hardly. Robin knew it deep in the core of her bones.

"I have to remember. I have to…" Images flashed across her thoughts so quickly, she couldn't hold onto any of them.

She felt vulnerable and terrified. *Come on, Robin, you remembered your name, you can remember the rest: your friends, where you work, maybe a boyfriend?*

Did she have one? She hoped so. He'd protect her, right?

"She's right. You're safe, Miss Strand," Detective Dunn said.

She glanced at him. His voice didn't calm her, not like Jake's. Detective Dunn was a bulky, tough-looking man with a permanent frown, and almost vicious glint to his eyes.

Oh, cry. You are so overreacting.

"Are you afraid of Jake?" Detective Dunn pushed. "You think he tried to hurt you?"

"No, I'm not afraid of him. I'm…" Robin shook her head and closed her eyes.

"Do you remember anything that can help us?" the detective said.

"Yes. No. I'm not sure how real it is."

"Real?"

She opened her eyes. "It looks like a dream, in my head. It could have happened, but maybe not. I'm sorry. They tell me I have amnesia." She fingered a gold locket at the base of her neck. "Sounds stupid."

"We're getting ready to move her to a room," the nurse said.

"I'll check back later," the detective said. "But I have to ask, are you sure Jake wasn't trying to hurt you?"

She thought it odd that he asked. "I'm sure."

"Even though you can't remember what happened?"

"What do you want from me?" Her voice went up an octave.

"Please," the nurse said to the detective. "We're trying to keep her calm."

"Sorry. I'll be close, ma'am."

She didn't care if Detective Dunn stayed close, but she hoped Jake would keep his word and be right outside. What was happening? Was she developing some kind of syndrome for the handsome stranger? Sure, why not? He was the only thing she remembered before waking up in the hospital.

With a sigh, she laid her head back against the pillow. The nurse checked the minor contusion on her head, probably the cause of her memory loss.

"I'd like to call someone," Robin said, then hesitated. "But I don't know who to call."

She sounded sad, even to her own ears, yet she didn't think she was a sad person.

"Here's your briefcase." The nurse placed it on Robin's lap. "I'll bet you've got an emergency number in your cell phone."

"Great, thanks."

"They'll be down shortly to take you to a room." The nurse wrote something on a chart and hovered beside Robin, probably afraid she'd have a complete mental breakdown if left alone.

Robin began the search of her messy briefcase. She dug and shuffled things around, but came up empty. No cell phone.

She zipped open a side pocket and found her wallet, keys, gum and lip gloss. She pulled out her driver's license. "At least I'll know where to tell the cab to drop me," she muttered.

The nurse shot her a sympathetic smile.

Gripping her briefcase to her chest like a security blanket, Robin inhaled, hoping the scent would trigger some kind of memory. She closed her eyes and sighed.

A few seconds later, someone cleared his throat. She opened her eyes and Jake stood there, not too close, offering a tentative smile. "I thought… I wanted to make sure you were okay. You looked scared before."

"Sir, you shouldn't be here," the nurse said.

"No, it's okay." Robin sat up a little and fought the urge to brush flyaway hair off her face. *Sheesh, girl, he's not interested in you that way.* Not to mention she must look like she'd just gone ten rounds in a boxing ring.

"I'm glad you came back," Robin said. "What happened tonight, to me?"

"We're not sure." He took a slight step closer, but just one. "I was outside the Chambers Building and saw you running. Something spooked you, big time."

"They think I saw a murder?"

"Yes, but they don't know for sure."

Robin attempted a smile. "It's a good thing you were there."

"Glad I could help."

A few seconds of awkward silence stretched between them as the nurse checked a monitor. Jake seemed uncomfortable, but Robin couldn't figure out why.

"Well, anyway," he said and turned.

Panic shot through her chest. "Are you leaving?"

He glanced back at her. "I wasn't going to, not until you're settled. If that's okay."

"Yes, very okay. I mean I'd rather you stay around if you've got

nothing better to do, which I'm sure you do, but if you didn't—"
She stopped herself. "Sorry. I'm rambling."

The nurse smiled as she checked Robin's IV.

"You've been through a lot tonight," Jake said. "You're allowed."

"Guys hate ramblers." She remembered that from somewhere.

"Not all guys." With a half smile he pointed to the door. "I'll be right outside that door."

"Thanks."

"No problem."

She liked Jake and wished he'd been a permanent part of her past. Then again, this could be part of a goofy syndrome that happens when someone is saved by another person.

A handsome man with gentle eyes.

That hit to your head really messed you up.

"I've got to check on another patient. I'll be right back, okay?" the nurse said.

"Sure."

But Robin was far from okay. She had to get a grip on her discombobulated brain and focus on the problem at hand: remembering.

She clutched her briefcase to her chest, closed her eyes, took a slow, deep breath, determined to remember. Instead, anxiety washed over her. Something important was happening soon, and she was in charge of a lot of people. Yet she'd be lucky if she could cross the street on her own. Her knee was banged up, her head was wonky, and she'd sprained her wrist when she fell to the ground.

You were very lucky.

She'd heard those words at least five times since they'd brought her in. Yes, it could have been so much worse. She considered thanking God for her good fortune, but stopped herself. Somehow she sensed He'd never answered her prayers before, so why give Him the credit?

"Miss Strand, how are you feeling?"

She opened her eyes to the back of a doctor in green scrubs. He was doing something, probably looking over her chart.

"I've been better," she said.

"I'm going to put something in your line to help you sleep tonight."

"Oh. Okay." The other doctor had said he didn't want to completely zonk her out. Oh well. Different doctors, different styles.

The doctor stood just behind her bed and fiddled with her IV. "A good night's sleep might help you move past the trauma."

"And help me remember?"

"You don't remember anything about what happened tonight?"

"No. Well, yes. I remembered the guy who helped me. That's good, right?"

"Remembering anything is good." He paused. "You don't remember what you witnessed in the office building?"

"What I witnessed?" she repeated, feeling suddenly cold. "No, I don't…" Her head felt like a lead weight sinking into the pillow.

"Rest, Miss Strand," he said, his voice sounding far away. "Everything will be fine."

The doctor turned to her, a surgical mask covering his face, except for his eyes.

Cold eyes she'd seen before.

"Death eyes," she whispered as unconsciousness swallowed her.

TWO

Jake should leave. There was nothing more he could do here. Even Ethan had told him to go home, that he'd done enough.

That look on Robin's face kept Jake glued to his chair in the waiting area. At first he thought she'd been terrified of him. Then, just now, she'd looked at him as if she needed him to protect her.

She was vulnerable and alone, and the only thing she remembered about her life before she'd woken up was Jake.

Ironic since they'd never even met.

"Who did you say your client was again?" Detective Dunn pressed.

"I didn't. I'd have to get his permission to share that with you."

"There's no attorney-client privilege here, Walters."

"True, but he asked me to keep it confidential and since he's paying my light bill at present..." Jake shrugged.

"How about I take you to the station and question you?"

"Why are you busting my chops?"

Jake eyed a doctor breezing out of the E.R. to the exit, still in his scrubs and face mask.

"I know you're furious about losing Edwards, but I'm not the bad guy here." Jake defended himself.

"Well, the least you did was chase the woman into traffic, ruining our chance of her IDing the perp."

Jake clenched his jaw against the frustration ripping through his chest. He felt bad enough without this guy twisting the knife deeper into his conscience.

"Look, I was there. It was a coincidence." Jake stood and paced a few feet away, beating back the guilt.

He'd never been able to defend Mom. He'd been scrawny as a kid, skinny and uncoordinated. It wasn't until he'd joined the service at eighteen that he'd developed his fighting skills and his muscular physique.

"I saw you go in there while I was on the phone," Dunn said. "What did you say to her?"

Jake was about to shoot the detective a mind-your-own-business retort when he was nearly taken down by two residents rushing past him. They flew into the examining area in a panic.

No. It couldn't be Robin. A doctor had just left and—

Instinct setting him on edge, Jake headed for the examining area. Dunn blocked him.

"Please get out of my way," Jake said, as calmly as possible. His heart raced at the thought of his worst fear coming true.

The killer walking right past him and Detective Dunn...

...and killing Robin Strand while they stood there, just outside the door.

"Where do you think you're going?" Dunn said.

Any second now the cuffs were coming out. Jake couldn't protect her if he was sitting in lockup.

"To check on the woman," Jake said.

"She's fine."

Another doctor and nurse scrambled past them into the E.R. as a Code Blue echoed through the hospital's PA system.

Jake glared at Detective Dunn. "She's not fine."

He stepped around Dunn and marched into the examining area. Medical staff shifted around Robin's bed in a mass of frantic motion.

"Still dropping," a nurse said. "Ninety over sixty."

Jake stepped closer. Robin looked pale and weak. He felt incredibly helpless. Like before, like all the times he couldn't protect Mom.

This woman, so young and vibrant, didn't deserve what had happened to her tonight. She didn't deserve to die because she'd been in the wrong place at the worst possible time.

But a few minutes ago she'd been fine, coherent and strong considering she'd woke with no memory and was probably terrified.

Dunn grabbed Jake's arm. "Let's go."

"She's dying," Jake shot over his shoulder.

Jake and Detective Dunn watched the medical team struggle to bring Robin back from the edge of death.

"What did you give her?" the doctor barked.

The resident rattled off some medications but Jake could hardly focus on what he was saying. Robin was dying. Right in front of him.

"Increase her IV fluids," the doctor said, then glanced at a monitor. The monitor stopped.

"Get me calcium chloride." The doctor started doing CPR as the nurse added something to Robin's IV.

"Look at the bizarre complexes on the heart monitor," the doctor said. "I'm guessing she got potassium chloride by accident."

By accident? Hardly. Jake was right. The killer had been here, inches away from Robin, sticking something in her IV to end her life.

He'd seen plenty of death during his time in the service but nothing like this. An innocent woman nearly killed twice in one night.

"What about—"

"Stop talking," the doctor interrupted his resident.

Jake's pulse pounded against his throat. He couldn't stop Dad from hitting his mom or prevent the cancer from killing her in the end. Nor could he stop little kids from being used as target practice in Iraq.

But he had honestly thought he could protect Robin Strand.

"Come on, Robin," a nurse whispered.

They all looked shell-shocked, like they were holding themselves personally responsible for her condition.

He knew the feeling.

Jake said a silent prayer, one that had seen him through the darkest days overseas.

"Eighty over fifty-five," the nurse said.

"Thatta girl," the doctor whispered, easing up on the CPR.

The numbers on the monitor continued to rise.

"Page me if her condition changes," the doctor said, then turned to the other resident. "Find out everything you can about her medical history."

"She has amnesia."

"Have the police help you." The doctor eyed Dunn. "I need her medical history ASAP."

"I'll get on it." Dunn grabbed Jake's arm and pulled him out of the examining area. "Sit." He motioned for Jake to sit in the waiting area.

Jake clenched his jaw and Dunn paced outside to make the call to track down everything he could on Robin. Jake was tempted to bust out of the hospital and do his own digging, but he wouldn't leave until he knew that she was safe.

He leaned forward in his seat and interlaced his fingers. He needed to talk to Ethan, tell him about the mystery doctor who had exited the room minutes before chaos erupted. The guy obviously gave her the potassium chloride that messed with her blood pressure.

Which meant whoever had tried to kill her wasn't going to stop. Yet it didn't seem like Detective Dunn was all that concerned about Robin's well-being. In Dunn's eyes she was a witness, a means to an end. That's all.

Jake hated feeling helpless and had promised himself never

to sink into that dark place again. He'd lost count of how many times he'd walked into it and out the other side.

With help from God.

He shoved the helplessness back and strategized ways to protect Robin. She was the key not only to a cop's murder but potentially to something bigger. Why else would a guy walk into a hospital, impersonate a doctor and spike her IV?

The question was, how far up the chain did it go? And how was Jake going to protect her if the cops were blocking him every step of the way?

An hour later, the glass doors slid open and a red-faced Ethan marched toward Jake. Jake knew that look, that I'm-frustrated-and-want-to-slug-something look.

Jake shifted in the vinyl chair.

"What happened?" Ethan said.

"Her blood pressure dropped and she nearly died," Jake explained.

"Where's Dunn?"

"I'm here."

Ethan turned to him. "Where were you when someone tried to kill my witness?"

"Making a call about the case. Just checked on the witness. She's stable. They're moving her to a room."

"You find anything out at the scene?" Jake asked.

"You're not a cop, Jake," Ethan said. "I can't talk to you about it."

Jake cocked his head in question but didn't challenge Ethan. He was under a ton of pressure and Jake didn't want to add to it.

"Dunn, call Monroe. He's working on the woman's background: school, hobbies, bank balances. Everything."

Dunn pulled out his phone and marched outside.

"You're not looking at her as a suspect, are you?" Jake asked his friend.

Ethan put his hand on Jake's shoulder. "Seriously, go home."

"Not happening." Jake eyed Ethan. "A doctor left the E.R. just before her B.P. dropped. Gut tells me he's the one who spiked her IV."

"Did you tell Dunn about this?"

"No."

"Good. Let's keep this between us."

"You don't trust your own men? You need to fill me in, buddy," Jake said.

"Not now. I'll call you later."

"I'll be here."

"Jake, seriously, this isn't your problem."

"The woman's here because of me, someone tried to kill her while I was sitting outside the door, and you just said you can't trust your own guys. It *is* my problem."

"I didn't say I didn't trust them. It's just…this is complicated. The chief of D's is breathing down my neck on this one, probably because Detective Edwards wasn't supposed to be at the Chambers Building tonight."

"Meaning?"

"I don't know," he snapped. "Was he dirty? Or doing undercover work someone isn't bothering to tell me or the chief about?" Ethan took a long, deep breath and exhaled. "Don't you have other clients who need you?"

"They pay me, they don't need me. Go find the shooter."

"As long as you're here, maybe I'll take Dunn back to the scene."

"Take him, please take him." Jake smiled.

They shook hands and Ethan went outside to confer with Detective Dunn.

In truth, Jake didn't have anything pressing to deal with. He was still getting his act together after his mom's death six months ago, going through her things, getting the house ready for sale. He was taking his time and slowly easing into his P.I. business.

Yet clients had conveniently appeared over the past few months when word got out that a former federal agent and army vet was offering his services as a private investigator. Jake had promised himself he'd be selective about his clients. He'd work with the fragile ones who were in trouble and didn't know where else to go.

Fragile, like Mom. He had taken a leave from work when he'd learned his mom had six months to live. He could finally be there for her, take care of her during her last months on earth. He felt he was finally making up for letting her down time after time growing up.

Yet she never saw it that way. She actually blamed herself for the abuse, which had driven Jake even crazier.

"Let it go," he whispered under his breath.

He'd been a good son in the end and now offered his services to clients who needed him most. He offered hope when they suffered from despair. That's where he did his best work. God's work.

The E.R. door swung open and a nurse glanced at Jake. "She's asking for you."

Jake pointed to his chest. "Me?"

"You're Jake, right?"

"Yeah."

"They're taking her upstairs in a minute, but she wanted to see you first."

With a nod, he followed the nurse and fought the urge to rush to Robin's bed.

He approached with caution, steeling himself against how she'd look. She'd almost died a few minutes ago.

The nurse pulled the curtain aside and Robin glanced up at him with tired, brown eyes. She looked worn out but much better than she had an hour ago.

"Hey, you look good," he offered.

"Don't lie. It's a bad way to start a relationship," she joked.

"And a sense of humor. Amazing."

"No, the bad guy luckily didn't kill that." She sighed and glanced at the nurse. "May I have a few minutes alone with Jake?"

"Sure." The nurse pulled the curtain closed to give them privacy.

"Look, I've heard things about you," Robin started, studying her fingers while she fiddled with the blanket.

"Don't believe everything you hear."

She glanced up. "What about the military background?"

"The hospital grapevine is pretty good."

"And you used to be a federal agent?"

"True. How did—"

"It doesn't matter. But I have a question—actually a favor—to ask, and I completely understand if the answer is no."

"Go for it."

She leveled him with desperate, cocoa-brown eyes. "I think I was almost killed tonight. Twice. I don't know who I am, or who I can trust. Is there any way you could like, be my bodyguard or something, until this is all over?"

"Sure, I'd be honored."

She tipped her chin. "You didn't even think about it."

"I don't have to."

She blinked, and a tear trailed down her cheek.

He fisted his hand, wanting to stroke her hair or hug her. But he knew better. He'd only break her.

"Wow, my luck is looking up." She swiped at her face with the back of her hand. "Sorry about the tears. I know guys hate that, too."

"Who are these guys you've been hanging out with?" he joked, trying to lighten the mood.

"I don't remember," she said with a slight smile.

The nurse pulled back the curtain. "Time to move her to a room."

"Where?" Jake asked.

"Three-fourteen."

He glanced at Robin. "I'll meet you up there."

She nodded and sighed as if everything was going to be okay. She was relying on him to protect her, save her from whatever threat planned to hound her until she was dead.

God, please let me be up to the task.

THREE

Where am I this time?

Robin opened her eyes and glanced across the room. Sunlight streamed through the curtains as she struggled to remember where she was. Right, she was in the hospital. Yet no flowers filled the window ledge, no balloons or notes from well-wishers.

Sadness settled in her chest. She felt so utterly alone and frightened, yet she knew she had friends. Her memories might be temporarily lost, but in her heart she knew some things as surely as she knew she was in a hospital bed.

Robin had friends and family who would be worried about her. If she could only figure out how to contact them.

"Can I see some ID?" Jake's voice echoed from her doorway. He was keeping guard outside her doorway, having promised to protect her.

"Who are you?" a woman challenged. Her voice sounded familiar.

"ID," Jake repeated.

A few seconds passed, then heels clapped against the vinyl flooring, and a cute blond woman came into view.

Jake stood beside her. "She says she's a friend from work."

The blonde rushed over and gave Robin a hug. Jake started to intercede and Robin waved him off. "It's okay."

There was something familiar about the woman, and Robin didn't feel frightened. Actually, she appreciated the hug.

Jake nodded and left them alone.

"Oh, my God." The blonde analyzed Robin's bruised check and bump on the head. "When I heard the gunshot, then nothing, I was up all night trying to track you down. I'm sorry it took me so long to get here."

"What time is it?"

"Three in the afternoon."

"You—" Robin hesitated "—heard the gunshot?"

"We were on the phone, remember?"

"No, actually. I'm memory-challenged at the moment."

"Oh, sweetie, I'm so sorry."

Another hug. Robin fought back tears.

The blonde looked at her. "We were on the phone. You were at work, and I ordered you to join us for dinner, then *bang!*"

Robin jerked. Closed her eyes.

"Sorry, that was insensitive." The blonde placed a hand on Robin's shoulder. "What happened?"

"I don't know. I—" she hesitated "—can't remember."

"Anything? I mean, you don't remember what happened last night?"

"Nope."

"Good." The woman sighed. "I mean who wants to remember seeing someone get shot, right?"

"Yeah, right, I guess." Robin clutched the blanket. "It's all one, big blob of nothing."

"That's probably normal."

Robin glanced at her friend. "I mean everything."

The blonde frowned. "You don't know me, do you?"

"I remember the sound of your voice, and you look familiar, but I don't remember your name. Sorry."

The blond woman shot Robin a sympathetic smile. "Don't be sorry. It'll come back. I'm Jenn. We work together." With a bright smile, she extended her hand, and they shook.

Robin liked this woman. She was bright and positive, and her presence eased the ball of anxiety in Robin's chest.

"I should call work and let them know you'll be out for a while," Jenn said.

"Where do I work?"

"You're an events planner for the Anna Marsh Pediatric Cancer Foundation. Tomorrow is the walkathon to raise money for pediatric cancer research."

Sadness washed over her. "I knew something big was happening."

"See? It's coming back to you. I'll call Ruth, the executive director. Where's your phone?"

"I think I lost it when…"

A scene flashed in her mind: *crawling on her hands and knees. Pitch black. The monster stalked her. Closing in. Would she make it to the door? Pull the fire alarm!*

"Robin?" Jenn said.

Robin glanced up. "I was remembering…something."

Jenn frowned with concern.

"Never mind. It's nothing," Robin said.

"And your phone?"

"I don't know where it is, but my briefcase is around here somewhere."

"I'll get it. Who else do you want me to call? Your parents?"

"Are they in Seattle?"

"Actually, they moved to Phoenix a few years ago."

"No, don't call them yet. I don't want to worry them. Just for now, let's keep this between you and me."

"Well, the group kind of knows. They were with me when I was talking to you. Trevor was so worried." Jenn winked.

"Trevor?"

"The guy you've been crushing on for the past three months. I could make up a playbill of people in your life to help you remember."

"That would be great."

"What's causing the memory loss?" Jenn said.

"Trauma to the brain. I banged my head when I hit the ground. They say it's a miracle I didn't sustain more serious injuries."

"No kidding." Jenn went into the closet and pulled out Robin's briefcase. "You want to…" She held the briefcase out to Robin.

"No, you go ahead."

Jenn rested it on the bed, dug around and pulled out a file folder. "This should have Ruth's home number. I'll give her a call. Oh, and it looks like you printed out the sign-up sheets. Want me to get those to her?"

"That would be wonderful."

"No problem. It's a bummer you lost your phone."

"Yeah." It probably had all her information, names and contact information, special dates and deadlines, and even personal information. She nibbled her lower lip. If she'd dropped it at the scene, the killer probably had it, which meant he might know everything about her.

"Hey, it'll be okay," Jenn said, sensing Robin's trepidation. "Here." Jenn pulled a small notepad out of the briefcase, wrote something down and handed it to Robin. "My contact info if you need something or remember anything and want to talk it out. Whatever."

Robin smiled as she eyed the notepaper. Jenn had written down her name, address and phone number, with the message, *Call me anytime!*

"If you want, I can stop by your apartment and bring back some things." Jenn said. "Stuff that'll make you feel better."

And help you remember. Robin heard the inference.

"Thanks," Robin said. "My keys should be in the briefcase."

Jenn dug them out just as a tall, serious-looking man with a crew cut stepped into the room. A scar ran across his right eyebrow. Did Robin know him?

"Ma'am, I'm going to have to ask you to leave," the guy said to Jenn.

"Who are you?" Jenn asked.

And where was Jake? Robin wondered.

"Detective Monroe, Seattle P.D." He flashed his badge.

A cop, an ally. Not a threat. Robin relaxed a little.

"Okay." Jenn glanced at Robin. "I'll be back later." Jenn smiled and left.

Narrowing his eyes, the detective took a step closer to her bed. Robin felt small and cornered.

"You can fool the rest of them with your amnesia ploy, but I know what's really going on."

"What are you talking about?"

"What'd you do, promise Cole a lead on a case?"

"I didn't promise anything, and I don't know what you're talking about."

"Why Cole? Huh? Was he onto something, so they sent you to lure him in?" He clenched his jaw as if he was about to snap.

"You'd better leave," she said, her voice trembling.

"Not until you give me something." He grabbed her wrist and cuffed it to the edge of the bed.

"What are you doing?" Her heart slammed against her chest.

"Making sure you stay put until I can get answers." He stalked around to the other side of the bed and poured her water. "Maybe this will help."

"I can't remember! Let me go!" She pulled on the handcuffs.

Caught. Snared. Stalked. About to be…killed?

She repeatedly pushed the nurse call button.

He closed in on her. No matter how far she leaned away, she couldn't escape his stale coffee breath or the look of hatred in his eyes. "Cut the nonsense, lady."

"Get away from her!"

* * *

Jake grabbed Detective Monroe's arm and yanked him away from Robin. Anger arced through Jake's chest at the look in her eyes. Terror didn't begin to describe what he saw there.

Monroe glared at Jake. "You're interfering with an ongoing investigation."

"And you're bullying a witness. This woman is a victim, not your perp."

"I'm not so sure." He eyed Robin.

She pulled on the handcuffs.

"She nearly died in the E.R.," Jake said. "Uncuff her and get out."

"Not until she answers some questions," Monroe said.

"I don't know anything!" she cried.

A young nurse rushed into the room. "What's going on in here?"

"Police, ma'am." Monroe flashed his badge. "I've been ordered to ask Miss Strand questions."

"She's not ready to answer your questions," Jake said.

Monroe glared at him. "You're a doctor now, Walters?"

"Stop it," the nurse ordered. "She's not up for visitors or interrogation. Now remove these cuffs and leave. Both of you."

Monroe fisted his hand, and Jake realized the guy was dangerously close to doing something he'd regret. There were few things worse than losing a brother in blue. Jake understood the man's emotional state but didn't condone it.

"Let's call Detective Beck," Jake said.

"You do that." But he didn't move to uncuff Robin.

"And I'm calling security," the nurse threatened.

Monroe snapped his glare from Jake and went around to release Robin. She turned away, her eyes connecting with Jake's. He offered a slight smile, wanting to let her know it would be okay. He wasn't going to let anything happen to her.

"We're not done," Monroe shot at Robin.

The nurse motioned for him to leave. "You, too," the nurse said to Jake.

"No. Can he stay?" Robin asked.

The nurse frowned. "For a few minutes."

Monroe stormed out with the nurse on his heels.

"You okay?" Jake asked.

"I've been better."

She had a resilience about her that fascinated him. A cop, one of the good guys, had threatened her. but she hadn't backed down.

"They think I was involved in the shooting?" she asked.

"They think you might have witnessed something. A police officer was killed tonight."

Her eyes widened. "And that cop thinks I shot him?"

"I doubt it, but cops get crazy when a fellow officer is killed."

"Yeah, he's crazy and wants answers." She sighed. "And my mind is a complete blank."

"It will come back to you, in time."

"I get the impression I don't have time."

Jake shoved his hands into his jacket pockets. He couldn't argue with her.

"Someone's after me," she said in a soft voice.

"We don't know that."

"But if I saw something…"

"You need to focus on healing. You're safe here."

"You're kidding, right? I almost died in the E.R., then a crazy cop handcuffs and interrogates me."

Jake took a step closer. "It won't happen again. I'm sorry I let Monroe question you."

"He's a cop. It's not like you could have stopped him."

"It doesn't matter who it is. You asked me for help. I'll make sure no one gets that close again."

She leaned back against the pillow but didn't look convinced.

A distant memory flashed to the surface to taunt Jake. *I won't let him hurt you again, Mommy.* But Jake had failed to keep that promise.

"You know the doctor in the E.R., the one who probably put something in my IV?" she said.

"Yeah?"

"I've seen him before."

"You recognized him?"

"Just his eyes." She hesitated. "Death Eyes."

The nurse came into the room and checked Robin's blood pressure. "Your few minutes is up," she said, not looking at Jake.

"How are her vitals?" Jake asked.

"Everything looks good." The nurse smiled at Robin.

With a nod, Jake started for the door.

"Wait, Jake?"

He turned to her.

"Thanks, for coming to the rescue."

"Don't mention it."

"Do you...?" She hesitated. "Would you want to sit in here?"

Robin glanced at the nurse.

"If it would make you feel better," the nurse said.

"It would." Robin motioned to a chair.

It hit a little too close to home, having recently spent months sitting beside Mom, but Jake read panic in Robin's eyes. She would feel better if he stayed close.

"Sure." With a nod, Jake collapsed in a corner chair where he had a clear view of the door.

The nurse finished up and left Robin and Jake alone.

Robin leaned against the pillow and eyed him. "Can I ask you something?"

"Sure."

"Why are you here?"

"Excuse me?" He sat up straight. Had she forgotten asking him to protect her?

"Don't look so worried. I remember asking you to stay," she said as if she'd read his mind. "I'm wondering why you came to the hospital with me in the first place."

Crossing his arms over his chest, he said, "I guess I feel responsible. It's my fault you ran into the street."

"You weren't trying to shoot me."

"No, but I frightened you, and you tore off to get away from me."

"I wish I could remember." She closed her eyes and pulled the blankets up to her chin.

The woman was a mess. Who wouldn't be? The hospital should be a safe place, a healing place. Instead, it had turned into a war zone where enemies hid in every corner from the E.R. to her hospital room.

Detective Monroe. A complete jerk. Jake couldn't believe the guy had gone after her like that, handcuffed her to the bed. What on earth was he thinking?

"I wish you could remember, too," Jake said.

With a sigh, she rolled onto her side, facing him. Wrapped in blankets, she looked childlike and fragile.

"I'm afraid of what comes next," she said in a soft voice.

"Don't be. Just rest. That's the best thing you can do for yourself."

She nodded and closed her eyes. He folded his hands behind his head and leaned back. This woman tapped into all his protective instincts from his mom, to his ex-girlfriend, to innocents in Iraq. He was overthinking again.

He glanced at the door as someone passed. That's what he should be focused on, not the tender beauty wrapped in white.

He suddenly wondered if this was his chance at redemption, his chance to make it right. He'd see Robin through to the end and make sure she wasn't another innocent victim of violence.

* * *

Robin awakened with a start, terrified all over again. She glanced around to get her bearings and spotted Jake in the corner of the dark room, asleep in the chair.

She hadn't slept well, tossing and turning, her thoughts driving her into a deeper sense of foreboding. She'd seen something she shouldn't have, and couldn't remember anything clearly enough to help the police find the killer.

Those buried memories were going to get her killed.

She didn't want to die. She had a lot to do, things to accomplish. Too bad she couldn't remember what they were.

A creaking sound from the doorway made her jackknife in bed. She squinted through the dark room toward the light in the hallway, but no one was there.

She was tempted to ask for a sleep aid, but didn't like taking drugs of any kind, even an over-the-counter pain reliever, although she'd accepted a few of those earlier to ease her pounding head.

Placing a hand to her heart to calm herself, she flopped back against the bed and eyed Jake, her self-proclaimed bodyguard. His arms were folded across his chest, his head tipped forward. Guilt snagged her insides. He looked so uncomfortable. She shouldn't have asked him to stay, but she didn't know who else to turn to. She needed someone's help, and so far Jake had been the only person in her life who seemed to be more concerned about Robin than the murder case.

The shrill sound of the phone made her jump. She grabbed it, not wanting it to awaken Jake. "Hello?" she whispered.

"Death Eyes is coming for you," a gravelly voice whispered.

She slammed the receiver, ripped out her IV and jumped out of bed, backing up against the wall.

"Robin?" Jake said, clearing his throat and sitting up. "What's wrong?"

"Phone," was all she could say.

The walls closed in. She wasn't even safe in the hospital. The cops considered her a suspect, the killer had spiked her IV, and although Jake was here, he didn't owe her anything. He could abandon her at any time.

She felt like a revolving duck at a carnival shooting gallery, ready to be picked off as she made the next turn.

Although much of her memory was lost, she knew she was a strong and determined woman. She was not going to be terrorized by a phantom and lie in bed waiting for him to finish the job.

"It's okay," Jake said, edging toward her. "Why don't you get back into bed?"

"And wait to be killed or arrested? No, thanks. I've got to get out of here."

She hobbled to the closet, her sore knee giving her a little trouble.

"Robin, be reasonable." Jake blocked her.

"Please get out of my way." She planted her hands on her hips.

He stepped aside. She grabbed the bag with her clothes and went into the bathroom. She caught a glimpse of herself in the mirror. Who was that woman?

"Very funny," she muttered. She recognized herself, she just didn't like what she saw staring back at her: a bruised and pathetic-looking woman.

"You are not pathetic. You're just hurt. And scared." She searched her briefcase and found her wallet. "Awesome." She had forty bucks and a few credit cards plus her driver's license with her address.

The cash was enough for a cab. She remembered what Jenn had written on the slip of paper: *Call me anytime!*

But it was the middle of the night, really not a good time to call a friend and ask for a ride. Robin could take a cab to Jenn's place, at least that way her friend wouldn't have to get dressed and drive to the hospital to get her.

Robin slipped on her pants and buttoned her dirt-smudged, cream-colored blouse. Her head was still foggy, but she was okay, surprisingly okay. She slung her briefcase over her shoulder and opened the bathroom door.

Her gaze locked on Jake's amazing blue-green eyes.

"Don't argue with me." Robin went to the bed and searched the table for Jenn's note.

"Why are you leaving?" he challenged.

"I can't sleep."

"Who was on the phone?"

She snatched Jenn's note off the floor and shoved it into her pocket. "It doesn't matter."

Robin stepped around Jake, marched to the door and glanced down the hall toward the nurse's station. A nurse sat at a desk with her back to Robin.

He stepped in front of her. "I wish you'd reconsider."

"Please get out of my way."

"A doctor should release you."

"I can't wait for a doctor." She walked around him and opened the stairwell door.

"It's not safe to go home," he said, following close behind her.

She gripped the railing as she climbed down the stairs, slowly, favoring her right leg. "It isn't safe here, either."

He stepped in front of her and blocked the door to the ground level. "What happened?" He narrowed his eyes as if trying to read her mind.

She gripped the strap of her briefcase. Besides Jenn, this stranger was the only person she could trust. "He called my hospital room."

"Who?"

"Death Eyes."

"How do you know it was him?"

"He identified himself."

"How did he know you called him that?"

"I think I whispered it before I passed out. What does it matter? He's coming for me, and I'm not waiting around to be killed!" She closed her eyes, embarrassed by her outburst.

Jake's warm, solid hand brushed against her sleeve. "It's okay. Take a deep breath. I'm not going to let anyone hurt you, remember?"

With a sigh, she opened her eyes. "I'd like to believe you, I really would. But let's be real. I don't know you. Why should you help me?"

"I've given you my word." He opened the door. "My car's in the garage."

Great, now she was going off with a strange man?

"You can drop me at Jenn's."

"Please stay close," Jake said, his hand on something inside his jacket. A gun? Did he expect Death Eyes to pop out from behind a car?

She hoped by morning the fog would lift from her brain, and she'd recall exactly what happened. At this point all she could remember were flashes of memory, frightening flashes.

She glanced at her briefcase and rubbed her fingers against the smooth leather. She remembered doing this before, brushing her hand across it while holding her cell phone to her ear.

Memories echoed in her brain.

I'm ordering you a longhorn burger as we speak.

Walking toward the elevators…noticing a light from an office spilling out into the hallway…she glanced right—

"Stop!" she gasped.

"Robin?"

She struggled to breathe, gripping Jake's jacket with trembling fingers, "I saw the light from the office. Someone was there."

"In the Chambers Building?"

She nodded, but words couldn't make it past her throat.

"It's okay." He glanced across the half-empty garage. "Let's get you out of here." He put his arm protectively around her shoulder and led her to a small pickup truck.

Robin couldn't stop trembling as the memory clawed at the edge of her mind, taunting her, terrorizing her with the unknown.

A bang made her shriek.

"Shh, it's okay. Someone just slammed a car door," Jake said, squeezing her shoulder.

As they approached the pickup, a security officer stepped in front of them. "Ma'am, are you okay?"

"I'm…I'm, no," she said wanting to destroy the memories circling her brain like crows over a dead animal.

"Sir, I'm going to have to ask you to step away from the woman," the security guard ordered.

"You don't understand—"

"The woman obviously feels threatened by you."

Jake released her and Robin felt utterly vulnerable all over again.

"Robin, stay close," Jake said.

The security guard stepped between them. "Sir, please keep your distance."

"She's suffering from a head injury."

"Hands on the car."

Jake turned and placed his hands to the roof of his truck. "Robin, it's okay."

He was being patted down and was still trying to take care of her.

"What's this?" The guard pulled a gun from inside Jake's jacket and waved it in his face.

She shivered at the sight of the black steel. A chill started deep in her bones and permeated her entire body to her fingertips.

"I'm a private investigator. I have a permit for that."

Robin had seen one of those before, black steel aimed at her…

She backed a few steps away from Jake and the guard as she fought back the memories.

A red stain spreading across the carpet…

Saturating a man's crisp, white shirt.

Her pulse raced as she turned away from the sight of the gun. She looked up just as blinding headlights pinned her in place.

The squeal of tires pierced her eardrums.

She couldn't move, couldn't cry out.

"Robin!" Jake shouted.

FOUR

Jake lunged at Robin and yanked her out of the way of the moving car. Blood pounding in his ears, he turned his back and held his breath.

The roar of the engine bounced off the low ceiling as the car clipped another car, then sped away. Jake glanced up to catch what he could of the plate number. The guard chased after the car, probably with the same idea.

The feel of Robin clinging to his shirt snapped Jake's attention back to the trembling woman in his arms.

"It's okay. Shh." He stroked her hair, held her against his chest. He couldn't remember ever comforting a woman like this. Was he doing it right?

"He tried to hit her," the guard said, marching up to them. "What was that about?"

"Call Detective Ethan Beck. He'll explain it."

Jake gave the guard Ethan's number. While the guard made the call, Jake opened the passenger door to the truck and placed his hands on Robin's shoulders.

"Why don't you get in the truck?" he said.

She nodded with a look of utter devastation. Her beautiful eyes were clouded with fear.

"Hey." He tipped her chin up with his forefinger. "You're okay. He's gone."

She absently shifted into the front seat. He started to shut the door.

"Wait," she said. "Can you…leave it open?"

"Sure, no problem."

The guard walked around the truck to Jake and held out his cell phone. "He wants to talk to you."

"Are we good?" Jake asked the guy.

"Yes."

"My gun?"

The guard slipped it from his belt and handed it to him.

Jake took the phone and stepped away from the truck. "Ethan, someone just tried to—"

"I know. Listen, I'm going to text you the address of a safe house. Get her there, ASAP. My guys are waiting."

"Are you sure you can trust them?"

"Yes. Just go with me on this, okay? I'll fill you in later."

"I got a partial plate on the vehicle that tried to run her down. Washington plate, starts with one-six-four. Honda Civic probably seven, eight years old."

"Thanks. I'm depending on you, buddy," Ethan said.

"So is Robin. She's asked me to stay close."

"Robin might be involved in something pretty nasty. Drop her off and drive away."

"You keep asking me to do that, but you know I won't."

"Jake—"

"Talk to you later." He ended the call and handed the phone to the security guard. "I've got to get her to a safe house."

"Right. Sorry about before."

"You were doing your job."

Jake went to the passenger side of his truck. Robin's eyes were closed. She leaned back against the headrest.

"Robin?"

She looked up, fear tinting her chocolate-brown eyes, and something pinched Jake's chest.

"I'm taking you to a safe house, okay?"

She nodded, clinging to her leather briefcase.

Jake shut the door and glanced across the parking garage. The guard was halfway to the elevator, but otherwise there was no movement. His shoulders knotted with tension. He got behind the wheel of his pickup and took a deep breath.

"It's going to be okay." He kept saying that and yet it never was okay. Everywhere Robin went it seemed like danger was lurking in the shadows, ready to jump out and attack her.

Kill her.

He shoved the car in gear and pulled out of the garage, gripping the steering wheel with more force than necessary. Would her attacker be waiting on a nearby side street? Tail them and make another attempt on her life?

"Can you talk to me?" she said.

"About what?"

"I don't care, you know, small talk? I'm spinning again and need to stop it."

"Spinning?" He headed north on State Route 99 and kept a keen eye on the rearview mirror.

"I get stuck in a bad head space and spin like a top. I'm afraid I'm going to have a full-blown anxiety attack."

"Don't beat yourself up for that. You've had more threats against your life in the last thirty hours than the average person has in two lifetimes."

She sighed and glanced out the window. Light rain tapped against the glass.

"Sorry, that didn't make you feel better, did it?" he said. "Okay, small talk." He searched his mind. "The Mariners look good this year."

She tipped her face to study him. "Tell me something about yourself."

He redirected his focus to the traffic ahead of them. "What do you know so far?"

"You're a war veteran and federal agent."

"Was a federal agent."

"You're too young to have retired."

"I took personal leave to help out my mom."

"So, now I know you're a good son."

He shrugged. If he'd really been good, he would have defended her long before the cancer took hold. He would have stood up for her instead of hiding when the old man swung his way through the house.

"You have brothers and sisters?" she asked.

"One sister. Older." Always absent. Jake understood. Amy had to take care of herself. She'd done pretty well in life, earned her degree, married a decent man and had kids. She'd settled in eastern Washington, far enough away to be safe from the old man.

"Your parents?" Robin asked.

"Old man's been gone for five years, and Mom passed in January. Cancer."

"I'm sorry."

"It's okay. She's in a better place."

"That expression never makes me feel better."

"You remember hearing it before?" He winked, trying to lighten the moment.

"Yeah, I guess I have."

A minute passed. She fidgeted next to him, and he guessed the silence made her uncomfortable.

"So," she started up again. "You took a leave of absence from…"

"Homeland Security."

"Do you intend to go back?"

"Probably not. I'm doing pretty well as a P.I. and private security."

"You mean, for me?"

"I've done private security for other people."

"How much do you charge?"

"Depends on the case."

"What about my case?"

"Don't worry about it."

"Jake—"

"Really. Don't. I figured *pro bono* work into my operating costs. I won't starve by helping you out."

"Are you…?" Robin hesitated.

"What?"

"Never mind."

"Aw, don't tease me like that."

"I was going to ask if your family will be upset with you for spending so much time protecting me."

"Nope."

"Your wife and children?"

"No wife. No children. Why did you think I was married?"

"You just seem the type."

"Yeah? What type is that?"

"The settling-down type."

"If there's one thing I've learned in my thirty-one years, it's never to assume you know someone."

He thought he knew Mom, but some days she was a mystery. After all, why would the woman stay with an abuser?

Cassandra, his near-fiancée, wasn't any easier to understand. She'd said she'd wait for him to return from his tour of duty. She'd said a lot of things that had turned out to be lies, but not everything. Like her accusation that he had violent tendencies. She'd hit the mark with that one.

"Why did you join the military?" Robin pushed.

He understood her need to keep talking, even if he was uncomfortable answering her questions.

"Couldn't afford college," he lied. He was offered a few scholarships, but he carried so much anger inside of him he figured he'd put his violent tendencies to good use and fight for his country, maybe exorcise some of his angst.

"Your turn," he said.

"I can't remember anything, remember?" She shook her head. "That sounded dumb."

He wanted to remind her she remembered something about last night, but the goal was to keep her calm, not upset her again by stirring up the memory of the man she called Death Eyes. He'd bring that up later, after she calmed down.

"I think you remember more than you think." He smiled, hoping to ease her anxiety. Maybe this was a bad idea, but he had to try. For her sake. "What's your favorite color?"

"Blue," she said, raising her eyebrows in shock. "How did I know that?"

"See, you do remember some things. How old are you?"

"Twenty-nine."

"Where do you live?"

"I can't tell you."

"Afraid I'm going to stalk you?"

"No, I saw my address on my driver's license. That would be cheating."

"You've got integrity. Add that to the list of things you know about yourself. How about, favorite movie?"

"Sound of Music."

"Book?"

She nibbled her thumbnail and gave it some thought. And for a few seconds she didn't look so scared. The tension eased in Jake's shoulders.

"Nope," she said. "I'm drawing a blank."

"Well, two out of three is good." He exited 99 and slowed at the stoplight. He punched the safe house address into his GPS and glanced in the rearview mirror. No cars behind him. He wasn't followed.

"Try another one," she said over the monotone voice of the GPS.

"Favorite food."

"Easy. Donuts from Pike Place Market."

"Powdered sugar or plain?"

"Powdered, definitely. I could eat those for breakfast, lunch and dinner."

"Not with that figure you can't." He shook his head. "Sorry."

She cracked a slight smile, at least he thought she did.

"Favorite TV show?" Jake continued.

"Castle."

"Brothers or sisters?"

Her smile faded and she gazed out the side window. The GPS directions echoed in the car between them.

"Robin?"

"How much longer to the safe house?"

"Five minutes."

He'd said something wrong and didn't even know what. Suddenly he felt the need to do his own background check on Robin to make sure he wouldn't walk into trouble again. The last thing he wanted was to upset her.

He followed the GPS directions and made a right, drove three blocks and made another right. They pulled up across the street from the address Ethan had given him. A light glowed behind the curtains in the small ranch.

He turned to her. "This is it."

She glanced at the house. "How long will I be here?"

"I'm not privy to that information. Sorry."

"Probably until this case is over, huh?" she whispered.

"Let's get you settled." Opening his door, he shot a glance one way up the street, then the other. It was nearly three in the morning, and the neighborhood was quiet. He came around the truck and offered his hand to steady Robin as she got out. She took it without hesitation.

"Thanks," she said.

He closed the door and he cupped her elbow as they crossed the street. She didn't pull away, and it felt natural to touch her like this.

"I was really lucky tonight," she said.

"How do you figure?"

She hesitated at the bottom of the porch steps and looked at him with worry in her eyes. "I'd hate to think what would have happened if you hadn't been at the Chambers Building."

"Then don't think about it. Come on, let's get you inside." He continued, glancing right and left across the neighborhood.

They started up the stairs and the door opened. Detective Monroe motioned them up the stairs as he scanned the neighborhood. "Let's go, let's go."

Robin stepped onto the porch and hesitated. "I'm not staying anywhere with you."

"We don't have time to discuss it. Get in the house."

"But you handcuffed me."

"I know. I'm sorry, okay? I'm a jerk."

"That's one word for it," Jake muttered.

Monroe motioned with his fingers. "I'll apologize more inside, okay?"

Robin looked at Jake for guidance. "Come on." He guided her in front of him toward the door. Once she crossed the threshold, Monroe blocked him.

"Sorry, Walters. Not you."

"No. Jake is protecting me," Robin argued.

Detective Dunn stepped out from the kitchen sipping a cup of coffee. "Yeah, he's done such a great job so far."

Jake tried to ignore the guy's comment, but it hit its mark. She'd been threatened twice while under Jake's unofficial protection.

"Beck told you to drop her off and leave," Monroe said to Jake. "That's what you're going to do."

Jake didn't want to get into a territorial fight with these guys. They were following orders and didn't like outsiders. He knew how it worked.

He also knew he'd made a promise to Robin.

"This isn't fair," Robin said.

"Look, Miss Strand," Monroe started. "We're going to protect you. You're involved in a criminal case and we don't want to risk screwing it up by involving civilians."

She crossed her arms over her chest. "You treated me like a suspect."

He sighed. "That was inappropriate. I was upset about Detective Edwards. I'm sorry you got the brunt of that. Truly."

It seemed genuine. Ethan told Jake he trusted these guys, and Jake didn't want to upset Robin with a turf war between him and the cops.

"He's right, Robin," Jake said. "It's their job to protect you. I have no jurisdiction here."

"I gave you jurisdiction." She cocked her chin up in defiance.

"Someone's got a case of transference," Detective Dunn said.

She glanced at him with furrowed eyebrows.

"Robin," Jake said to get her attention.

She refocused on Jake and he looked straight into her eyes.

"Remember what I promised?"

"Yes."

"I keep my promises."

Understanding dawned in her eyes. She understood that although he was leaving her at the house with the detectives, he wouldn't be far. Transference or not, he'd given his word.

"So, we're good?" Monroe said, looking from Jake to Robin.

"I guess," she said.

"Good night." Monroe shut the door in Jake's face.

Shoving his hands into his pockets, Jake walked down the steps to his car. He'd move it in case the cops looked out the window to make sure he'd left. Still, he wanted Robin to see him, to be assured by his presence.

Man, you're just feeding into her psychosis. Which is what it was, right? Detective Dunn had nailed it: she'd developed a healthy case of transference and was looking up to Jake as her protector.

He couldn't blame her after everything she'd been through.

However, he didn't think it was transference as much as it was her way of depending on someone who'd been steady and solid since her accident and memory loss. It made sense she'd cling to the one person who'd helped her from the beginning.

Fine, as long as they both knew that's all it was.

He got in the truck and drove around the block. He strategically parked at the cross street with a good view of the bedrooms in the back of the house. He had a feeling Robin would choose private space over sitting in the living room with the detectives.

Settling against the leather seat, he tried to relax, yet stayed alert. He'd need a clear head if he was going to keep an eye on Robin while flying under law enforcement's radar and being invisible.

Then again, he was a master at being invisible. He'd had years of practice.

Robin glanced around the messy living room. File folders and papers fanned across a dining table that was cluttered with coffee cups, paper plates with half-eaten sandwiches and bags of chips.

Detective Monroe received a text and went to open something on his laptop.

"We weren't expecting you until later," Detective Dunn said in an apologetic tone.

"I couldn't stay at the hospital."

"Yeah, I hate those places, too," he offered.

He was being nice. She appreciated it but still didn't trust the cops. They were focused on finding the killer and didn't care who they hurt in the process.

"Rockwell is such a clown!" Detective Monroe yelled at the computer screen. "Did you see his latest rant?"

"Stop torturing yourself," Dunn said.

"Who's a jerk?" Robin asked.

"Bill Rockwell," Detective Dunn said. "He's running for

mayor and using police corruption as his platform. I hate to think how Edwards's death is going to fuel his cause if we find out Edwards was dirty."

"He wasn't dirty." Monroe got up and stormed into the kitchen.

Dunn nodded apologetically at Robin. "We're all a little tense."

"Yeah, tell me about it."

"You want to watch TV or something?" he asked.

"No, I'm kinda tired."

"Then I'll show you to your room." He escorted her down a short hallway. "Here." He opened the door to a bedroom with a twin bed, nightstand and dresser.

"Thanks." She clung to her leather briefcase, the only personal belonging she had left. Worse, her clothes were dirty and torn from the accident.

She felt like a rag doll torn at the seams.

"We'll be in the living room if you need anything," Detective Dunn said.

"Thanks." She'd be polite to Detective Dunn, but nothing would change the fact she only trusted Jake.

I keep my promises.

"Bathroom's down the hall on the left," he said. "Fresh towels in the cabinet."

With a nod, he went back into the living room. She shut the door and studied her surroundings. Plain, beige, barren.

Sadness washed over her. She was not a beige person, was she? She didn't think so. She flopped down on the bed. What if, when she did remember who she was, she didn't like herself?

"Forget it. You've got bigger problems than not liking yourself." *Yeah, like being the target of a killer.*

Anxiety spread across her chest. "Not helpful."

She fought back the panic, turned off the overhead light and went to the window. She peered outside, knowing Jake was out there somewhere, close enough to protect her.

Then again, maybe he'd just said that to make her feel better. No. For some strange reason, she knew if he gave his word he'd keep it.

"Transference, huh?" she whispered.

Whatever. She didn't care what they called it. Having a former soldier and federal agent on her side had to be a good thing. She peered through her neighbor's backyard, but didn't see Jake's truck.

She took it on faith that Jake was out there, keeping an eye on the house. On faith? Melancholy settled low in her belly. She stretched out on the stiff, plaid bedspread and clutched her briefcase to her chest.

She began cataloging what she needed to do next. In a few hours, she'd call Jenn and tell her where to bring her clothes, plus get the cheat sheet. That would be a huge help. Maybe it was time to call her parents? Instinct told her that was a bad idea, that they'd been through enough.

Instinct was pretty much all she had going for her. She hoped it hadn't short-circuited along with her memory and was leading her astray.

Clinging to her briefcase, she took a deep breath and focused on going back to sleep. Jake said it would be okay, and she believed him.

All Robin could think about the next day was the walkathon. She should have been there, rallying the participants, cheering them on. Instead, she spent the day in a small house with detectives.

When they weren't asking her questions, they were in the kitchen whispering to each other. Probably discussing the case and their primary witness, who refused to cooperate.

Her muscles were stiff from the accident and her mind was still foggy, so she spent much of Sunday in her room.

Her room. The thought of living here for an extended period of time pulled her down into a funk.

No, she was a fighter. She changed the direction of her thoughts and focused on Jake. She had to believe he was still out there, keeping an eye on things. The thought gave her comfort.

"I just want this day to be over," she whispered. She wanted this whole nightmare to be over.

Around ten Sunday night, Robin stretched out on the twin bed. Exhaling slowly, she pictured the ocean; waves washing up against the sand, the sun warming her skin as she lay on a beach in shorts and a tank top. Had she been there before? Didn't matter. The image gave her a sense of peace.

She drifted off, imagining herself floating on a raft in the ocean, the rocking sensation easing the tension in her muscles. In the distance, she heard children laughing: the sounds of summer playtime on the beach. She smiled and opened her eyes.

The beach was littered with sun worshippers, dressed in colorful bathing suits, pitching sun umbrellas and lying on multicolored beach towels.

In the midst of the group stood a single man dressed in black.

He pointed something in her direction—

Bang!

Robin cried out and sat up. She glanced around the room and remembered where she was and how she'd gotten there. She was in the safe house. Everything was okay. She glanced at the clock on the nightstand. It read 2:30. She'd just had a nightmare.

"Cover the back!" a man shouted from the living room.

Pounding footsteps, then, "How did they find us?"

Bang! Bang!

"Officer down! Officer Down! Five-Six-Seven North—"

The bedroom door burst open. "You okay?" Detective Dunn said. "Uh!" He gasped, gripped his shoulder and fell to his knees.

She hesitated.

"Run!" Detective Dunn shouted.

She lunged for the window and shoved it open. If she stayed here, Death Eyes would surely find her.

She swallowed the panic flooding her mouth and climbed through the window. She dropped a few feet to the ground and jerked upright, ready to sprint.

A man grabbed her shoulders. "Don't move."

FIVE

"It's Jake," he whispered into her ear. His warm breath calmed her frantic heartbeat. "Look at me."

She turned around and lost herself in his blue-green eyes. It was really Jake.

He placed his forefinger to his lips, and she nodded that she understood. With a steady hand, he guided her away from the window, and she clung to his leather jacket. It reminded her of the briefcase. Now she'd lost that, too.

Jake turned to aim his gun at the house and shifted her behind him. The squeal of sirens pierced the quiet night.

With deliberate steps, Jake backed away from the house, shielding Robin. The wail of sirens grew louder as emergency vehicles closed in. The sound did nothing to calm her.

Once out of sight of the safe house, he motioned her through the neighbor's yard. She walked ahead, clutching her shirt as a chill crept across her shoulders.

"My car's over there," Jake said, motioning to the cross street.

"Where are we going?"

"Not sure yet." He continually scanned the perimeter and ducked when he spotted squad cars racing toward them. "Stay down."

He crouched down and she did the same, clinging to his arm. She pressed her forehead against the soft leather and struggled to stay sane and focused. She could easily fall apart right now. Not a good idea if she wanted to live.

She had to. She had responsibilities, things to do, to finish.

"Okay, let's go." They scrambled through another yard and raced to the truck. He shut her door, flipped up his collar against the rain and came around to the driver's side. His angry expression would have frightened her if she didn't know him.

Come on, girl. You don't *know him.*

He got behind the wheel. "Scoot down, so you're out of sight."

Since the truck had a bench seat, she could lie down, the top of her head touching his jacket. She interlaced her fingers and took a deep breath.

He pulled away from the curb and glanced down. "Good idea."

"What?"

"Prayer never hurts."

She was about to tell him she wasn't praying but stopped herself. Was it such a bad thing to ask for divine help?

Yes, it was.

"Where are we going?" she asked.

"Not sure yet. I need to talk to Ethan."

"Who?"

"My friend, Detective Beck."

"You think the other detectives are…okay?"

"I…" He hesitated. "I hope so."

Which meant he suspected what she did, too: the cops weren't okay. She didn't like the surly Detective Monroe, but he didn't deserve to be shot because he was protecting her.

"How did they find you?" Jake muttered. Then he slapped his palm against the steering wheel. "I couldn't even…" His voice trailed off.

"What?"

"I couldn't help them. I had to choose between you and the cops. I chose you."

"Because you'd promised," she said.

"And because you were the more vulnerable target." He clenched his jaw. "I've gotta believe those guys can defend themselves."

"Did you see who shot at us?"

"No. He came from the other end of the street. I can't figure it out…" He paused. "Unless… Where's your briefcase?"

"Back at the house."

"Good."

"Why good?"

"I'm thinking they planted a tracking device in your briefcase when you were at the hospital. That's how they found you."

She sighed and closed her eyes. She hated feeling terrified and vulnerable.

"It's safe to sit up now," he said.

She straightened and glanced out the window. "Why is this happening to me?"

"It's not your fault."

"Thanks, but that doesn't make me feel better."

"We'll get through it. Trust me." He shot her a comforting smile and pressed a number on his cell phone. "Ethan, it's Jake…I know. I've got her. I'll take her someplace safe…I agree. I will."

Jake rolled down his window and tossed the phone across the street.

"That bad, huh?" Robin said.

"I had to toss the phone in case they're tracking the GPS."

"Why would they track you?"

"I've been your shadow since the accident. I'm deep into this now."

Guilt snagged her conscience. "I'm sorry."

"For what?" He shot her a sideways glance.

"That I dragged you into this."

"You didn't drag me into anything. I want to help you. No guilt, promise?"

"Okay. What happens now?"

"We find a safe place and disappear for a while. We're on our own, for the time being anyway."

"What about the police?"

"Ethan isn't sure who he can trust. No one but his men knew you were going to the safe house and, until he finds a tracking device in your briefcase, he needs to consider he's got a bad cop on his payroll."

"Yikes."

"In the meantime, he's given me permission to take you someplace safe. He doesn't even want to know our location."

"Where are we going?"

"A small town on the peninsula called Port Whisper. Have you heard of it?"

"No."

"You'll like it." He shot a glance into the rearview mirror, unclenched his jaw. "It's a quiet little town."

She hugged herself, and a shiver crawled up her spine.

"We'll get you some warm clothes as soon as we can," Jake said.

"Thanks, but I left my wallet back at the house."

"I'll cover it."

"But—"

"No arguments. We'll call it a loan." He smiled, and she struggled to smile back, but couldn't. "It's going to take a ferry ride plus three hours to get there so why don't you get some rest?"

"Every time I fall asleep, something bad happens."

"Not this time. It's just you and me. No hospital, no cops."

She nodded and lay down on the bench seat. Would she survive the next twenty-four hours? She wasn't sure, but she knew one thing: she had a better chance with Jake than with the police.

He flipped on the radio to a classical station. The soft melody drifted across the car, soothing her just a bit. She interlaced her cold fingers and found herself looking for strength from somewhere, anywhere.

Prayer never hurts.

His words made her angry and sad. Yet, right now, prayer seemed like a good thing to do. She interlaced her fingers.

God in heaven, please help me.

Four hours later, Jake pulled into the town of Port Whisper. He'd called ahead to let Caroline know he'd be arriving with a friend.

A female friend.

Caroline Ross was his mother's closest friend, and had been gracious about being awakened at five in the morning by his phone call. She had teased him about bringing a girlfriend to meet his auntie Caroline, but he'd made it clear this was a work-related relationship.

Robin was in trouble, not unlike his mother had been.

Caroline's tone grew serious as she said she'd have fresh squeezed juice and warm scones ready when they arrived. She'd helped Jake's mom when she'd needed to escape her abusive husband. Mom would pack up Jake and Amy and head to Port Whisper, not telling Jake's dad where they were going. Jake and Amy would hang out at the community playground or race boats at the dock, while Auntie Caroline tended to Mom. Mom had called it girl talk and had said it would bore the kids. In reality, she hadn't wanted the kids to see her break down in tears.

Jake had a feeling she had done a lot of crying with her friend.

All Caroline had to hear was that Jake's friend, Robin, was in the same kind of trouble as Mom. He was sure Caroline would have a full spread ready for them, plus she'd probably put aside the most private, well-decorated room with the softest linens in the house for Robin. The tourist season hadn't picked up yet, so she said only two rooms out of ten were occupied.

A good thing. Jake hoped to stay as anonymous as possible.

He asked Caroline to put him in a room near Robin's, and she said that would not be a problem. They could have two rooms on the top floor, overlooking the town. That's where she'd put Mom, way up in a corner where she'd felt safe and protected. More than once he'd caught Mom frowning as she'd gazed out the window across town, looking for Dad's Lincoln to pull into the driveway.

But he never came. The Port Whisper Inn had been their secret, and Dad had never figured out the location of their refuge. The three of them had taken a break from the war zone at home and had enjoyed the innocence of small town life. He and Amy, pretending to be like normal kids from a happy home, had actually made friends with the locals. Back at home, they kept to themselves, didn't let anyone get close. Well, except Ethan. That kid had shoved his way into Jake's life, and although they had never talked about it, Ethan knew something had been going on in the Walterses' house.

Ethan hadn't judged Jake. He'd offered friendship. They'd even taken Ethan to Port Whisper a few times. Those were the best times of Jake's childhood as he and Ethan had explored the state park, climbed trees and discovered hidden caves. Jake had dreamed of winning great battles in Port Whisper, of defeating Dad and saving Mom.

While Jake had dreamed of saving Mom from Dad, Caroline had boosted Mom's courage. Only it had never been enough. Caroline hadn't been able to convince Mom to leave the old man. Jake had lost count of how many times she'd promised to leave him.

He pulled the truck out of sight behind The Port Whisper Inn and glanced down at Robin, who slept soundly on the seat next to him. He considered it a compliment that she felt so safe with him.

"Robin?" he said, brushing her dark brown hair off her face. "We're here."

She didn't wake up, and he was enjoying stroking her hair a

little too much. He tapped her shoulder and cleared his throat. "Time to wake up."

"Huh?" She sat up and glanced out the passenger window. "Where…?"

"The Port Whisper Inn. We'll be safe here." He got out and opened her door. "You need a minute to get your bearings?"

"No. No, I'm okay." She stepped out of the truck and her leg gave out.

"Whoa, there." He sat her on the truck seat. "Knee's pretty banged up, huh?"

"No, I'm still a little foggy. Feel like I've been run over by a truck."

"You only slept a few hours in the car. You could use another few."

"What time is it?"

"About seven. Caroline has rooms ready for us. Come on." He slipped an arm beneath her legs, hoisted her into his arms and carried her to the front steps. She wrapped her arms around his neck and buried her face in his shoulder. He reminded himself she'd be clinging to any man who had protected her like Jake had.

The front door swung open as he stepped onto the porch. Caroline opened her arms and greeted them.

"Jake, you look wonderful."

He doubted it, but Caroline was always such a positive person.

"Is she still asleep?" Caroline eyed Robin.

"No, just having trouble walking," Jake said.

Robin glanced at Caroline. "Had a run in with a car yesterday, and my leg's a bit sore."

"Well, come in. I have scones and juice all ready."

Jake took Robin straight to the kitchen and seated her at the table.

"Usually my guests eat in the dining room, but Jake's like family, so he makes himself at home in my kitchen." Caroline breezed around the pale blue kitchen like she floated on air. Jake knew she loved serving guests, baking—and helping people.

"Robin, this is Caroline Ross. Caroline, Robin Strand."

The women shook hands. "Lovely to meet you, Robin. What's your tea preference, or do you drink coffee?"

"Actually, I hate to be rude, but I'm still worn out, would you mind if I rested first?"

"Of course not. Everything will keep." Caroline pulled two keys out of her pocket and offered them to Jake. "You're upstairs in the Lily and Daffodil rooms."

The same rooms they'd stayed in when Jake was a kid. He hesitated before taking them.

"Jake?" Caroline said. "I have other rooms if you'd prefer."

"It's fine." He put the keys in his pocket, then reached down to pick up Robin.

She put up her hand. "I will not let you carry me up a flight of stairs."

"I've carried heavier things for longer distances."

She made a face. Had he offended her?

"Thanks, macho man, but no. Let's see if the leg's working." Robin put pressure on the leg, and Jake gripped her arm. She looked up at him with a wry smile. "I think I'm good."

She was more than good; she was adorable. He broke eye contact and started for the stairs. *Watch it, buddy. You already know she's developing inappropriate feelings. You don't want to compound that mistake.*

"Hey, I wouldn't mind an escort," Robin said.

Jake turned back to her and noticed she was gripping the chair for support. Okay, so her leg was working, but it wasn't one hundred percent. "Right, sorry."

As he offered his hand, Caroline shot him a knowing grin. She knew Jake and Amy as well as his own mom had, and she'd sensed his attraction to Robin and his subsequent awkwardness.

"Ready?" he said.

"Yep." Gripping Jake's arm for support, Robin shuffled toward the stairs.

"I really don't have a problem carrying you," he said.

She shot him a not-on-your-life-buddy look, and he couldn't help but smile. It was a slow ascent, but they finally made it to the second floor.

"The rooms are down there on the right." He pointed.

"You stayed here a lot?"

"It was our home away from home."

"Caroline acts like she's your second mom."

Jake paused in front of Robin's room. "She pretty much was."

He opened her door, holding his breath. This had been Mom's room with the window seat overlooking the grounds, metal claw bathtub and dressing table where Mom had sat and brushed her hair with a faraway look in her eye.

It didn't ignite the painful memories he'd expected, perhaps because Caroline had updated it with an armoire complete with TV and cable for a laptop. Ah, technology.

Yet the room was still decorated in pale colors, lace pillow covers, and a few antique pieces to give it character.

"This is wonderful," Robin said, awe coloring her voice.

"Glad you like it." He ambled to the window and remembered sitting right here, pretending to be the sentry assigned to keep watch for the monster.

"What are you looking at?" she asked, her voice soft.

Did she sense he was reliving demons of the past?

"It's a charming town, lots to do. My sister and I used to climb trees in the state park and have stick races in the creek. There's something about nature that makes sense of the world, ya know?"

What are you rambling about, Jake? You're either tired or so taken with this girl that you're opening up and blathering on about stuff she isn't interested in.

She needs you to keep her alive. That's it.

"Did you take vacations when you were a kid?" he asked.

When she didn't answer, he glanced at the bed. She'd fallen asleep on top of the down comforter, her hands clutching a small, decorative pillow.

Jake wandered to the bed and dropped a blanket over her body. "Sweet dreams."

He went back downstairs where he found a teenage boy sitting at the kitchen table, staring at a muffin on his plate.

"Good morning," Jake said.

"You the military hero?" the kid said, not looking up.

He had brown, scraggly hair that fell across his forehead and wore a beat up T-shirt.

"I served in the army," Jake said, sitting across the table from him.

"Jake, meet my oldest grandson, Steven," Caroline said, coming into the kitchen from the backyard.

Jake extended his hand.

"Sketch for short," the kid said.

Caroline shook her head in obvious disapproval of his nickname and poured a cup of coffee. Sketch didn't offer to shake Jake's hand. Instead, he put out his fist. Jake made a fist, and they bumped knuckles, a teenager's classic greeting.

"Good to meet you, Sketch."

The kid smiled, victorious that Jake had used his preferred name.

Caroline slid a mug of coffee in front of Jake. "It's so good to see you." She kissed Jake's cheek. "See, he's a military hero, and he lets me kiss him."

Sketch rolled his eyes and Jake bit back a smile. She turned back to the stove to pull a pan of muffins out of the oven.

"So, Sketch, school's out already?" Jake asked.

"For me, it is."

"Sweetie, why don't you take your muffin outside? It's really nice out this morning."

"What's the big deal? I was kicked out of school, so what?"

With a compassionate frown, Caroline started toward him. "Honey, I didn't mean—"

"I've gotta check on Mack." Sketch grabbed the muffin from his plate and rushed out the back door.

Caroline shifted onto a chair at the table and warmed her hands around a cup of tea. "Sorry about that."

"No, I'm sorry," Jake said. "I wasn't very good at keeping in touch. Mom told me Olivia had two kids, but I didn't know about, well…"

"My grandson being kicked out of school? I didn't know, either, until recently. He's a smart boy, truly brilliant. But he's had a hard time since his father left, and his stepdad, well, he doesn't have the patience."

"That's too bad. Where's Olivia?"

"She's at a nurse's convention in Portland so I've got the kids for a week. She and her new husband, Paul, have a son, Mack. He's just five. You'll see him sooner or later, I'm sure." She took a bite of a muffin and dabbed her lips with a napkin. "Enough about my family. Tell me more about Robin."

"I really shouldn't be involving you in this."

"Nonsense. Unburden your heart a bit."

He sipped his coffee and placed the cup on the table. "She witnessed a shooting last night, and there have been two, maybe three, attempts on her life since then."

"Poor girl."

"I wouldn't have brought her here, but I didn't know where else to go. I left her at a safe house and she was almost killed. My detective buddy, Ethan, is on the case."

"Your friend from grade school?"

"You've got a great memory."

"He was a nice boy."

"Yeah, well, he's trying to sort stuff out, but in the meantime…"

"In the meantime, the inn is your refuge." She paused. "As always."

"Thanks. You can't know how much…" He couldn't finish the sentence. Words didn't come close to describing how grateful he was to this woman.

"I know. And I'm glad you came back." She stood. "Now, it goes without saying I won't be charging you for the rooms."

"No, Caroline, I insist."

She put up her hand to silence him. "Instead, you'll make it up to me by doing some work around the inn. My handyman's on a sailing trip with his brothers and won't be back until next week. How about it?"

"I'd be honored." He glanced at the ceiling, worried about Robin, not wanting her to wake up in a strange place and get spooked.

"I'll take care of Robin," she said as if she'd read his mind. "You know I'm good at that."

He smiled and stood. "I'm not an electrician or anything."

"Don't need one of those. What I need is someone to unlock my shed outside. I think the key's bent. Here." She handed it to him. "If it doesn't open, feel free to bust it with the tire iron from the back porch."

"I've got some tools in my truck. I might be able to pick it."

"That would be great. I stored my best rose clippers in the shed and need to do some pruning."

"No problem." Jake went outside and unlocked the cab on his truck. He flipped it open and dug around, looking for the right tools to pick the broken lock. He was tired himself, having driven most of the day. But the adrenaline hadn't worn off yet, and he doubted it would as long as he was responsible for keeping Robin safe.

"Hey, you! Hands where I can see them!"

SIX

They couldn't have tracked him to Port Whisper. No way, no how. Jake slowly raised his hands and turned to find a local cop standing there, tapping his baton against his hand. He looked young, too young to be responsible for protecting the citizens of Port Whisper.

"Name, rank and serial number," the cop said.

"Excuse me?"

The cop burst out laughing and clipped the baton to his belt. "Jake, it's me. Morgan."

Jake slowly lowered his hands and narrowed his eyes. "Morgan?"

Morgan Wright, Jake and Ethan had been inseparable during Jake's time in Port Whisper.

"I'm chief of police, just like Dad."

Jake and Morgan shook hands, and Jake pulled the cop into a quick hug. "I can't believe it," Jake said. "I didn't recognize you."

Morgan had been a short, chubby kid with an infectious sense of humor.

"Yeah, no more jelly belly." Morgan patted his flat stomach. "Went away to college but found my way back here. I heard you got away, too."

Jake ignored the double meaning of Morgan's words. Jake and Amy had been very careful not to expose their real situation to anyone in Port Whisper. They didn't want to taint their retreat with the violence.

"Yep, did two tours of duty, got my degree and joined Homeland Security," Jake said.

"Sounds more exciting than stolen bikes and festival security."

"Excitement is overrated."

"Caroline called this morning and said you were coming back. Listen, I heard about your Mom. I'm sorry, truly. She deserved better."

Jake sucked in a quick breath. "Thanks."

"Caroline told me you brought a female with you." He smiled.

"Yeah, listen. About that—"

"No." Morgan put up his hands. "None of my business. I know."

The same words Jake had uttered when Morgan had asked about Jake's dad when they were kids.

"Actually," Jake started, hoping this was a smart thing to do. "I could use your help with this one. The woman's a witness to a murder in Seattle. I'm her unofficial bodyguard."

"Why isn't she in police custody?"

"She was. The safe house was compromised, and she was almost killed. We're laying low until it's safe to go back. Ethan's the lead detective on the case. I wish I could call him, but I can't risk the killer tracing us here."

"You could use my phone."

"Can't risk using any phone that could be traced to cell towers in the area."

"Makes sense."

"Was wondering if you could keep an eye out for strange visitors to town? She's suffering from amnesia, but things come back in flashes. She refers to her attacker as Death Eyes, so the guy must be creepy-looking."

"I'll do what I can." He paused and smiled at Jake. "It's good to see you. We'll have to catch up later. I've got to meet the mayor for coffee."

"Everything okay?"

"Yeah, yeah. Just the usual maintenance. Let me give you my number in case you need anything." Morgan pulled out a business card and jotted his personal number on the back.

They shook hands. "Good to see you, buddy," Jake said.

"You, too. Stay out of trouble." Morgan winked, got in his Jeep and left.

Things were looking up. Jake had the local law enforcement on his side, and no one knew where he and Robin were hiding out, not even Ethan. Although he'd probably figure it out if he found a sane moment to think about it.

Still, Jake knew E would never expose Jake and Robin's location, not until he'd sorted through this mess and figured out whom he could trust.

He grabbed his toolbox from the truck and headed to the shed to work on Caroline's lock. As he strode across the property, he took a deep breath and pretended, just for a second, that he was a normal guy, doing normal maintenance work on his house.

Old habits die hard. He'd pretended to be a normal kid with a happy home life during their visits to Port Whisper. It had eased the tension that had lodged in his chest and made it impossible to breathe at home with Monster Dad hovering in the next room.

Jake shook it off as he stepped up to the shed. He kneeled, pulled the key from his pocket and gave it a try.

"Mack broke it," Sketch said, stepping around the side of the shed.

"How'd he do that?"

"Tried to pick the lock with a stick. He was convinced there's a scooter in there."

"A scooter, huh?" Jake fiddled with the lock, but the kid was right. The key was worthless.

"Does your grandma know he broke the key?"

"Nah, didn't want to get him in trouble."

"You're a good brother."

Jake searched his toolbox for something long and thin to try and dig the stick out of the lock.

"I can help, ya know," Sketch said.

"I think I got it."

"No, I mean if you want to call your cop friend."

Jake paused and looked up at the kid. "You shouldn't listen to other people's conversations."

"Do you want my help or not?" He leaned against the shed.

"Depends. Does it involve breaking the law?"

"I don't think so."

"Okay. Then yes. After I bust into this shed."

"And you accuse me of breaking the law," Sketch muttered and walked away. "Come find me when you're ready. Command Center is in the basement."

Jake watched the kid disappear into the house. Sketch was not only bored but obviously fighting angst of his own, not unlike Jake had as a kid.

His gaze drifted to the porch, then up to the window overlooking the gardens. Robin's window. He wondered if she slept soundly, or if nightmares haunted her.

Don't wonder. You're getting too close, too fast. Was there a term for his side of the transference pendulum, he wondered? Better yet, were there preventive measures? Because he surely needed to distance himself from the emotions stirring in his gut whenever he imagined Robin's big, brown eyes or wounded expression.

What he wouldn't give for some distance. But he'd made a promise. And Jake did his best to keep his promises.

Robin inhaled the sweet scent of lilacs and a sense of peace washed over her. Waking from a fitful sleep of threatening images—running, screaming, racing away from danger—Robin welcomed the comforting scent that surrounded her like a soft, cotton blanket. She blinked and opened her eyes to the sight of the purple flowers in a china vase on her bedside table.

She instantly remembered where she was; at the inn, hiding out with Jake. Although her body still ached from the accident, she'd awakened with a renewed sense of purpose, determined to heal both mentally and physically from her ordeal.

As she sat up, she realized a blanket had been carefully tucked around her body, the flowers positioned just right so she'd enjoy the fragrance, and a crystal glass filled with water was within reach.

Thoughtful. Had Jake put the items there or had Caroline? Robin smiled to herself, feeling cared for...

For once.

That niggling pain started in her stomach again. She couldn't identify what it was, or why it twisted her tummy in knots whenever she thought about being taken care of. It was almost as if she'd been abandoned in her past, left to fend for herself, and the knot was sadness about missing out on the love from a nurturing family.

"If you think about this all day, you'll give yourself a headache," she scolded herself. It would come back to her in time, and when it did, she'd deal with it.

In the meantime, she had to gather her strength and stand up for herself.

She slid off the bed, thankful that her knee hurt a little less than it had a few hours ago. That's when they'd arrived, right? She glanced at a wall clock. It read one-fifteen. She'd been asleep for six hours.

Then her gaze caught on a sticky note on the closet. She wandered across the room and read the note:

You'll find temporary clothes inside the closet. See you at lunch—Caroline.

Caroline was a special woman, indeed. Robin felt an instant connection to her, and trust.

Robin found soft towels draped over a heated towel bar in the bathroom. She quickly showered. Although she was tempted to soak in the tub, she wanted to see Jake, because she had to know the status of their situation.

Really? Is that why you can't bear to be away from him for hours at a time?

Half an hour later, she'd dressed in a pair of sweats, T-shirt and a fleece jacket that was a size too big, but close enough. She wrapped her wet hair in a bun and locked her room. As she passed the Daffodil Room she glanced through the open doorway. Jake was stretched out diagonally across the bed, one arm draped over his eyes as if blocking the sunlight. Even asleep, he looked strong and competent.

He'd saved her life. Three times. Her heartbeat quickened at the thought. She wished she could return the favor, but the truth was she'd never come close to repaying him for saving her.

She shut his door to keep his room quiet and allow him to sleep. The guy probably left his door open in order to listen for danger if it passed on its way to Robin's room.

He was keeping her safe, even as he slept.

She wondered if anyone had ever cared so much about her. Surely she'd had a boyfriend or best girlfriend, right? Jenn seemed to fit that description. She'd offered to bring clothes back to the hospital and call Robin's parents. She'd have to explain where she'd gone once this ordeal was over. Whenever that was...

Robin went downstairs into the kitchen where she found Caroline making lunch.

"You're awake," Caroline said with a bright smile. "How did you sleep, sweetheart?"

"Great, thanks."

"Glad you found the clothes. You're about my daughter's size, and she had a bag of giveaways to drop off."

"Thanks."

"Grilled cheese and tomato sandwich or chicken salad?" Caroline offered.

"Grilled cheese and tomato, please." Robin shifted into a chair.

The back door swung open and a little boy rushed through the kitchen. "Grilled cheese, please." He sat across from Robin and studied his Toy Story plate. "Buzz Lightyear rules!" He picked up his plate, waved it like a flying saucer, and made engine noises.

"Mack, say hi to our guest, Miss Robin."

The little boy hesitated. "Hi, Miss Robin. Are you here for grilled cheese and tomato?"

"Yes, sir. Is it good?"

"It's the best in the West!" The little boy continued using his plate as a spaceship.

"Mack's one of my grandsons," Caroline explained.

"He's adorable."

"You think so? Are you adorable, Mackie?" Caroline tousled Mack's hair and he grinned.

Something ached in Robin's chest.

"What's for lunch?" Jake said, coming into the kitchen and sitting next to Robin.

"You were asleep," Robin said.

"Not asleep. Just zoned out for a few minutes."

"He had a busy morning," Caroline said.

"Really?" Robin studied Jake.

"He went shopping for supplies for your makeover, broke into my shed, and almost got arrested."

Robin sat up straight, but Jake waved off her concern. "The police chief is an old friend and was messing with me."

Robin relaxed. "Oh."

A few minutes later, Caroline served Jake, Robin and Mack their sandwiches and placed a colorful fruit plate, filled with watermelon, strawberries and grapes, in the center of the table. "Mackie, use the fork, not your fingers."

Caroline turned back to the counter, and, with a mischievous twinkle in his eye, Mack reached over with his fingers to snap a slice of watermelon. Jake stabbed it with a fork and dropped it on Mack's plate.

"Thanks!" Mack said, shoving the watermelon in his mouth.

Robin took a bite of her sandwich. The cheese practically melted on her tongue. She closed her eyes and enjoyed the taste that reminded her of childhood and innocence.

"As good as Market donuts?" Jake teased.

She opened her eyes and caught him smiling at her.

The basement door popped open, and a teenage boy stuck his head out. "Mack, bring me my sandwich when you're done with lunch. And war hero—" he nodded at Jake "—my offer's still open."

The door closed and Robin looked at Jake.

"That's Sketch, Caroline's older grandson," Jake explained.

"He's socially challenged," Caroline joked, but Robin sensed concern. "What offer, Jake?"

"He overheard me telling Morgan I want to contact Ethan about the case."

"Speaking of which, may I use your phone, Caroline?" Robin asked.

"No," Jake said.

"Wait. No?" Robin eyed him.

"We have to be really careful, Robin. No calls to friends or family or anyone they might be watching."

"Not even from a pay phone?"

"If they've got them under surveillance, it will give them the general location. We can't risk it."

"Who are *they?*" Caroline asked, joining them at the table.

"We're not sure, yet," Jake said. "Which is why I need to talk to Ethan."

"I'd really like to let Jenn know I'm okay," Robin said. "She's probably freaked out."

"Let's wait until we figure out a way to communicate safely, okay?" Jake said.

Robin nodded, feeling cut off from the only person she had a connection to in her former life. She realized she was completely dependent on Jake, yet it felt…okay.

"You've got a case of dissociative amnesia?" Caroline said matter-of-factly.

"Is that what they call it?"

"Cooper Fritz had a bout of it last year when his boat collided with a speed boat."

"What happened?" Robin asked.

"He recovered all his memories eventually, but most of them came back in a few weeks. It became a town project to help him along with sensory stimulation. You know—bake him his favorite pie, take him to his favorite places, give him whittling projects. He was a champion whittler before the accident."

"Did it help?" Robin asked.

"It did, actually."

Robin glanced hopefully at Jake.

"I'm game," he said. "We'll do a Google search after lunch and see how it works."

While they finished their lunch, Caroline updated Jake about the town, who'd moved in, who'd moved away and what new buildings were under construction.

Robin felt normal for a few minutes, like she wasn't a witness to murder or the target of a killer. She enjoyed the feeling of a home, even when Mack spilled his juice. If only spilled juice was the worst of her worries.

"Hello? Anyone here?" a man called from the front of the house.

Jake looked at Caroline. She stood, brushing her hands on her apron. "I don't have anyone scheduled to check in for three days. Wait here. It could just be a drop-in."

She left the kitchen and shut the door behind her.

Mack grabbed a plate with a sandwich from the counter, loaded it with fruit then carried it to the basement door.

"Hey, Mack, let me get the door for you." Jake grabbed a

bag off the counter, opened the door, and motioned for Robin to follow him into the basement.

They climbed the steep steps, Robin holding on to the railing for support, while Mack bounded down the steps with ease. She felt suddenly old and fragile.

When she stepped onto the cement floor, Jake steadied her with a hand on her arm.

"Thanks buddy," Sketch said when Mack slid the plate next to his computer.

"Can I? Can I?" Mack asked, pointing to an old computer system on a desk a few feet away.

"Go for it," Sketch said, not taking his eyes off his computer screen. "So, war hero, like my command center, complete with escape door?" He pointed to cellar doors leading outside.

"Impressive."

"I got something for your girlfriend on memory stimulation."

"Wait a sec," Robin said. "You weren't even there when we were talking about my amnesia."

"Looks like psychotherapy is a possible strategy, although memory doesn't necessarily return during the session," he said, ignoring her comment. "It can return randomly when the patient is feeling safe in her own home." He glanced at Robin. "Make that our home." He turned back to the computer. "There's also a theory that if you relive a memory it might trigger something, which clears the fog. If all else fails, there's always hypnosis, or Sodium Amytal which puts you in a semi-hypnotic state."

"Who are you?" Robin teased.

Sketch shrugged. "Just a kid who got kicked out of high school. What brought you down to the Command Center?"

"Your grandmother had some unexpected guests," Jake said.

"Happens all the time." Sketch rolled his eyes.

Jake motioned to the bag in his hand. "You got a bathroom down here? We need to change Robin's looks."

"Yeah, behind the furnace. Need help?"

"I got it, thanks."

Robin stepped around computer equipment and milk crates filled with vinyl record albums and made her way to the bathroom. She was mildly surprised how clean it was for a young man's bathroom.

Mom, Kyle's bathroom is totally gross!

She hesitated before stepping into the bathroom. Kyle, Kyle is…who?

"Robin?" Jake asked.

She shook it off. "Just nervous about what you're planning to do."

"A haircut and color job?"

"My hair," she whispered, pulling it out from the bun. She glanced at Jake. "We need to save what you cut off."

"Why?"

"We just do," she squeaked.

"Sure, okay." He looked at her sideways.

"I think…I think I'm planning to do something important with it."

"Like donate it?"

She held his gaze. "Love."

"Excuse me?"

"Locks of Love," she whispered. "I think I was going to donate my hair."

"You're remembering. That's great, Robin."

She nodded and stood in front of the mirror.

"I'm going to cut it so you can put it behind your ears, but it'll be above your shoulders. Is that good?"

"I guess."

"You can always have it fixed by a professional when this is over."

Would it ever be over? Right now, it didn't feel like it.

"Go for it." She closed her eyes and heard him pull something out of the bag, probably scissors.

But it wasn't. He expertly avoided the tender spot on the back of her head as he slid a brush through her hair. She tensed at first, then relaxed. It was a soft and comforting touch. She couldn't remember anyone doing this for her, not a parent or a girlfriend. As Jake's gentle touch filled her heart with melancholy, she grew anxious about remembering her past.

Sketch stepped into the doorway. "Gran says not to worry. The visitors were a couple looking for a romantic getaway."

"Great, thanks," Jake said.

"This place would be perfect for a romantic getaway," Robin said, but she hadn't meant to utter the words. She was so relaxed from Jake brushing her hair, that her censor was off and her guard down.

After a few more minutes, he stopped brushing and tugged slightly. She heard a snip, then another. This had to be done. It was a small sacrifice to save her life. She kept her eyes closed and tried thinking of something else, anything else. Unfortunately, the image of Detective Dunn being shot in front of her pushed its way ahead of other, calming mental images.

"Do you like your room?" Jake asked, almost as if he'd felt her trepidation and wanted to distract her.

"It's lovely, especially waking up to the lilacs on my nightstand."

"I was hoping you'd like them."

"You put them there?"

"Yep." He let go of her hair and brushed it a few times. "Okay, cut's done."

She opened her eyes and looked at the blunt cut. She was pretty sure a stylist would have taken twenty minutes to do what Jake just did in five.

He scooped up the clippings and put them into a bag. "For Locks of Love," he said. He pointed to a box of hair color on the sink. "Now we need to change the color. Ever been a blonde?" He pursed his lips. "Sorry, you probably don't remember."

"It's okay." She smiled. "I'm guessing blond wasn't my style."

"You're amazing, you know that?"

"Why? Because I let a man cut my hair?"

"Because you're being such a good sport about all this. I know how women are about their looks."

"And you know this how?"

"I have a sister."

He put on plastic gloves and read the directions. He mixed a powder with a liquid and the stench made her gag, so she reached over and turned on the bathroom fan.

"Sorry about the smell. We'll have to leave it on for a good twenty minutes since your hair's dark," he said.

"You're the expert."

She sat on the toilet seat and closed her eyes. He squirted the color along her hairline, then rubbed it into her scalp and squeezed it down the longer strands.

A phone rang in the distance and Robin realized how life moved along, regardless of the fact that she'd lost her memories and was being threatened by a killer. Phones still rang, and Caroline was upstairs probably taking a reservation for another guest.

Robin loved the feel of the inn and the cozy furniture in the living room, roaring fire in the fireplace, the pillow-top bed and grounds peppered with a variety of colorful flowers.

"Not bad for my first time," he said, sitting on the edge of the tub and ripping off his gloves.

She opened her eyes. "Thanks."

"You may not be thanking me once you see the end result."

"I'm alive, and I'm safe. Nothing else matters, does it?"

"No, I guess not," he said, glancing at the tile floor.

"What is it?" Robin sensed something was bothering Jake.

Sketch tapped on the door and handed Jake a phone. "It's for you."

SEVEN

Jake stared at the phone as if it were a hand grenade. There's no way anyone could have found them in Port Whisper, which meant whoever was calling was on a fishing trip, hoping to hook Jake with a phone call.

Jake grabbed the receiver from Sketch and hung up. "We're gonna have to go," Jake said. "I'll pack up while we wait for the bleach to work on your hair."

The phone rang again, and Jake handed it to Sketch. "Don't answer."

"Gran will."

It rang twice and stopped. The basement door opened. "Sketch, is Jake down there?"

Sketch eyed Jake and shrugged.

Jake went to the bottom of the stairs and made a slashing motion under his chin, hoping Caroline would get the message. Instead, she came downstairs and handed him the phone. "It's your friend, Ethan."

It could be anyone pretending to be Ethan. Everyone knew he and Jake were friends.

But it was too late. Caroline had already exposed his location, and he didn't want to make her feel bad about it.

Jake took the phone and Caroline went back upstairs.

"Hello?" Jake said.

"Thank God you're okay."

"Ethan?"

"I'm at a pay phone out of my district to avoid anyone tracing the call."

"How did you find me?"

"I'm a good detective."

In other words, he knew Jake well enough to know where he'd go to hide out. Old habits died hard. They'd done plenty of hiding out in Port Whisper as kids.

"Good enough to figure out what happened last night at the safe house?" Jake asked.

"Not yet, and the Chief of D's is crazed over this case, but then we've got a dead cop, Dunn took a bullet in the shoulder and Monroe…"

"What?"

"He's in critical condition, Jake. They don't know if he'll make it."

"I'm sorry." And he was. He wished he could have helped the cops, but he had to protect Robin. She was his primary concern.

"It's bad. I don't know who I can trust."

"Did you check her briefcase for a tracking device?"

"It was clean. Jake, the Chief of D's keeps asking why Robin was at the Chambers Building on a Friday night."

Jake glanced across the basement at Robin, hair saturated with bleach, sitting next to Mack as he played a computer game.

"Meaning what?" Jake said.

"We have to keep our options open."

"You keep them open. I'm following my gut on this."

"And I have to follow procedure."

"Which is?"

He feared Ethan was going to demand Jake bring Robin back to Seattle.

"Look, I trust you more than anyone in my own department, as crazy as that sounds. But I'm feeling pressure from above, probably because of that idiot mayoral candidate Bill Rockwell. He's making his platform on police corruption and if Edwards's death is related to illegal activity that supports Rockwell's case."

"Do you really think Edwards was dirty?"

"I don't know. But Jake…" He hesitated and Jake steeled himself against Ethan's next words. "The Chief of D's suggested Robin was involved in the murder of Detective Edwards and in exposing the safe house this morning."

"She's a victim of circumstance, Ethan."

"Just stay close to her. I'll let you know when it's safe to return."

"Are you going to expose our location?"

"No. I can't risk them finding her and killing her—or you, for that matter. I am truly sorry for involving you in this."

"Do we even know what *this* is?"

"I'd hate to speculate."

"Ethan, it's me."

Ethan's heavy sigh filled the line. "We suspect a drug distribution ring is moving a narcotic similar to oxycodone into Seattle under the radar. But now…"

"Now what?"

"Looks like Detective Edwards was taking money to look the other way."

"Then why kill him?"

"Maybe he grew a conscience, I don't know. Our Media Department released a statement that he was killed while working an off-duty security job at the Chambers Building. We don't want the drug organization figuring out we're onto them. We want to wrap this thing up before the DEA takes it away from us."

"Do you think any of your other cops were involved?"

"I don't think so. If Robin could remember what she saw, that might give me a clue where to look."

"Have you done a complete background on her yet?"

"Yep."

"Can you email it to me from a secure source?"

"I'll use my brother's email account."

"If I know more about her, I'll be able to coach her through this. She's terrified of something, and not just the shooting."

"Okay, I gotta get back."

"Be careful."

"Yep."

Jake hung up and glanced across the basement. Sketch was absorbed in something on his computer, and Robin played a video game with Mack.

When it was the little boy's turn, Robin glanced at Jake and studied him with curious eyes. He instantly shoved aside the thought that this woman could be involved in the drug-smuggling operation.

More likely, someone was using her as a diversion, making it look like she was involved to draw attention away from the real criminal.

"Do we have to pack up?" she asked with disappointment in her voice.

"No, we're still safe here. Ethan won't expose our location."

"What did he say?"

Jake motioned her toward the bathroom. "One thing at a time. Let's check your hair, then we'll talk."

She whispered something to Mack, and he giggled. As she walked toward the bathroom, he realized she was a natural with kids. Remorse settled heavy in his chest. A family was not in the cards for Jake. He'd never risk losing his temper and realizing he was just like the old man.

He checked her hair color. "Looks good. Put your head in the sink, and I'll wash your hair," he said.

"I'm not an invalid." She shook her head and gripped the ceramic basin. "I'm sorry. I hate feeling this dependent."

"Understandable."

"What did Ethan say?"

"Let's talk about it upstairs, away from the kids."

She leaned over the sink and turned the water on.

Jake grabbed shampoo from the shower and stood by, waiting for direction. She was growing impatient with her limitations and life-threatening situation. She probably wanted to feel like she had control over something, even if it was simply being able to wash her hair.

"Shampoo, please," her muffled voice said.

He squirted shampoo onto her lightened hair and rubbed it into her scalp. He considered Sketch's suggestions about memory stimulation, hypnosis or drug therapy. But they were in a small town with limited resources. Still, Caroline mentioned a man who'd suffered from dissociative amnesia. Maybe they'd try the hypnosis route.

"Feels good," she said. "Got any conditioner?"

"Hang on." He grabbed a bottle of conditioner from the shower and applied it on her hair.

"I got it," she said, massaging her scalp with her fingers.

They needed a plan other than sitting in the basement, waiting for someone to find them.

In his head, he clicked off what to do next: teach Robin self-defense, help her remember, stay concealed. Luckily, the second-floor rooms had a direct outdoor stairway down to the ground level so they could come and go without being noticed by other guests.

They'd changed her appearance and now had to focus on Jake. He'd have to dye his hair black and buy some new clothes. A dress shirt and tie would certainly change his typical appearance.

Robin turned off the water and towel-dried her hair. "The moment of truth." She removed the towel and studied her hair. "Huh. Not bad. At least it didn't turn out orange."

"It definitely makes you look different," Jake said to her reflection the mirror.

"Yes, but cuter or dorkier?" Her brown eyes snapped up to meet his. "Sorry, that was a weird question."

"Not weird." He handed her a brush and they walked out of the bathroom. "But for the record? Definitely cuter."

With a smile, she blushed and started up the stairs. Sketch glanced at Jake and gave him a thumbs-up.

Jake shook his head. What was he thinking flirting with the woman? No, he wasn't flirting. He'd meant it as a compliment, sensing she needed a boost in a big way. Could she really not know how adorable she was?

Stop thinking about nonsense. Your goal is to keep her safe, not build up her ego.

Caroline turned to them as they stepped into the kitchen. "Look at you," she said to Robin. "That's a lovely color."

"Thanks."

"How's Ethan?" Caroline asked Jake.

"Worried. This case is complicated."

"How can I help?"

"I may need to find someone who does hypnosis."

"My friend, Rosalie, at the health center has done some hypnosis for weight loss."

"You trust her?"

"Absolutely. Let me call her and see if she'd do a private session here at the inn."

Wandering into the front hall, Caroline pulled out her cell and made the call.

Jake studied Robin, who was more quiet than usual. "You okay?"

"I guess."

"Robin?"

Her brown eyes snapped to him.

"This only works if we're both completely honest with each other. Come on, what's bothering you?"

"Kyle."

"Who's Kyle?"

"I don't know. But I feel sad when I say his name."

"You said his name before you passed out at the scene of the accident."

"You think it's a boyfriend?" She looked puzzled at the thought.

"Ethan's almost done with your background check. He'll email it to me, and we'll go from there, okay?"

She nodded, nibbling at her lower lip. "I may not remember anything, but I know I'm not usually this fragile."

He wanted to cross the kitchen and pull her into an embrace. That would only seriously confuse things, especially if this Kyle she was starting to remember was, in fact, a boyfriend.

Caroline breezed back into the kitchen. "I left a message for Rosalie. I'm sure she'll call as soon as she gets a break."

"I'd better head out and pick up some clothes for us," Jake said.

Robin gripped his arm. "You're leaving?"

"I have a better idea," Caroline said. "I'll go shopping for both of you. I could use the break. It's been forever since I shopped for a man. Steven is offended by everything I buy him."

"I could use collared shirts and ties. Maybe a sport coat, something different than my usual leather jacket."

"I'll start at the secondhand shop in town. Worst case scenario, I'll drive over to Fred Meyer."

"You sure?" Jake said.

"I welcome the break from dishes and linens. It's the perfect time to scoot away. My two guests are off sailing for the day."

"Thanks," Jake said. "And if it's convenient, maybe pick up some glasses for Robin, reading glasses, lowest strength possible."

He pulled out his wallet and handed her cash, knowing a credit card was deadly.

"You could use some more clothes, too," Caroline said to Robin. "What do you like, dear?"

"Sundresses, jeans, cotton shirts. Size eight. I like blues and greens." She glanced at Jake and cracked a hint of a smile as if proud of herself for remembering.

Caroline grabbed her purse and put Jake's cash into a side

pocket. "Can you two man the phone while I'm gone? Steven gets impatient if a potential guest asks too many questions."

"Sure, and I could clean up the breakfast dishes," Robin said.

"No, that's okay."

"Really, it would feel good to be productive."

"I'd appreciate that."

Caroline called little Mack upstairs and convinced him to leave his older brother and join her on a grand adventure.

"See you later."

Caroline and Mack left and Jake poured himself a cup of coffee.

Robin turned to him with her damp, blond hair and determined expression. "Okay, we're alone. What did Ethan say? Are the detectives who guarded me last night okay?"

Jake glanced into his coffee. "Dunn's going to be okay, but Detective Monroe was critically wounded. They don't know if he'll make it."

"Because of me," Robin whispered.

Jake took a step toward her. "None of this is your fault."

She turned on the water and started washing dishes. "Wish I believed that."

So did Jake. He needed her focused, determined to remember and put this whole thing behind her.

"What else did he say?" she pressed.

"He's no closer to figuring out why Detective Edwards was at your building last night. They're wondering why you were there so late?"

She snapped her gaze to meet his. "There was a big walkathon today, a fundraiser."

"You remember?"

"No," she eyed a flowered plate in her hand. "Jenn told me when she stopped by the hospital. I guess you're starting to wonder about me, too, aren't you?"

"No, but the more information we have, the more successful we'll be in resolving this case sooner than later."

"They suspect me, don't they?"

Now wasn't the time to keep the truth from her, even if it was hard to hear.

"Ethan's superiors are questioning your involvement, yes."

"How can I prove my innocence if I can't even remember?"

"You will." He grabbed a towel to dry the dishes.

"I'm not sure I'm comfortable with the whole hypnosis thing," she said.

He sensed something terrified her about her past, something that happened way before the shooting.

"Only as a last resort," Jake assured. "I think we can stimulate your memories in other ways. When Ethan sends over a copy of your background report, it might help spark something."

"I wish I could remember on my own."

"How about some free association? It could shake loose whatever's blocking your memory."

"I guess it's worth a try."

"Let's sit outside," he offered.

Jake called down to Sketch. "Hey, Sketch, Robin and I will be on the back porch, but we've got the phone okay?"

"I can answer it."

"Thanks, but we want to earn our stay."

"Whatever," Sketch called back.

Jake grabbed the cordless phone and followed Robin out into the bright sunshine.

"Before we start on the memory stimulation, I'd like to teach you a few moves," Jake said as they wandered onto the porch.

"Moves?"

"Self-defense, in case you find yourself alone in a threatening situation."

Panic rushed through Robin's body. "But you'll always be with me, right?"

"That's the plan, but, just in case, it would be good for you to be able to defend yourself. I'm going to teach you something called the palm heel strike. It's simple, but effective. First, get into a ready position by fisting your hands like this." Jake held his arms at a ninety-degree angle and fisted his hands.

Robin imitated him.

"Good. Now, the objective is to hit spots with no muscular protection. Just think in terms of three—three strikes to three vulnerable areas using the heel of your palm as your weapon. First is the nose."

He pretended to hit her in the nose with the heel of his palm. "Right, left, right. You try."

She aimed the heel of her palm toward his nose.

"Put your shoulder into it. That's where the power comes from. Try again. One, two, three."

With a nod, she tried again. One, two, three.

"Great, then you go for the ribs. Turn your hand sideways to get maximum impact from the heel of your palm."

Focused on his black T-shirt, she aimed and snapped her arm, one, two, and on three she accidentally made contact with his hard chest.

"Sorry, I don't want to hurt you," Robin said.

"You won't. But you've got to practice, so you can do it without thinking."

They practiced the self-defense moves for a good ten minutes, Jake gently correcting her when she didn't put enough shoulder force into it. He was a wonderful teacher, supportive and encouraging. She just wished he was teaching her about something else, like sailing, instead of self-defense.

"You're looking good," he said with a smile.

She reminded herself he was complimenting her technique.

"Let's take a break before the memory exercises," he said, settling in a wood Adirondack chair.

She sat beside him and calmed the adrenaline rushing through her body from the self-defense lesson. She hoped she'd never have to use the palm heel strike.

She hoped Jake would stay close until this was all over.

Gazing across the colorful gardens and soaking in the warm, spring breeze, Robin wanted to pretend all was right with the world, that she wasn't being hunted by a killer and her brain was functioning just fine.

But the fact Jake had just taught her how to strategically hit an attacker blew that wish out of her mind.

Her mind. That's what this was all about. Trying to remember, trying to work past the fear of the trauma and recall what had happened last night.

"Ready?" Jake said.

"Yep."

"I'll say a word and you say whatever comes to mind. No thinking about it. There's no wrong answer, got it?"

She nodded and fiddled with the cord of her fleece.

"Cat," Jake said.

"Dog."

"Power."

"Hungry."

"Tree."

"Moss," she answered.

"Work."

"Stressful."

He chuckled at that one.

"Love," he said.

"Grief." She snapped her gaze to meet his. He offered a tender smile, but she read the pity there. And she hated it—the pity, the dread, and the cloud that always followed her.

"Mother," he tried again.

"Father."

"Grass."

"Green."

"Boyfriend."

Gone. She didn't speak the word, but the pain of loss welled up in her throat. She walked to the edge of the porch, gripping the white railing.

"What is it?" Jake said.

"I don't want to do this anymore."

"Robin?" He stepped up beside her and placed his hand on her shoulder.

Her racing heartbeat slowed as she took comfort in his warm touch.

"A part of me is afraid to remember." She glanced into his eyes. "I'm not sure I can handle it."

"You mean the shooting or something else?"

She looked away, across the colorful garden. There was hope in the blooming flowers, hope cultivated by the hand of a gardener who loved tending the soil.

The phone rang, startling her out of her moment. "I should answer," she said.

He handed her the phone. "Port Whisper Inn, may I help you?"

"Caroline?"

"No, this is her friend." Robin paused, realizing sharing her name could put her in danger. "How can I help you?" She stepped into the kitchen, looking for a notepad to write down a message.

"This is Rosalie. She called asking if I could help her friend." She hesitated. "With a project. Could you tell her I can stop by this afternoon around three, if that's good?"

"I'll give her the message."

"Great, thanks."

Robin hit End and glanced at Jake. "The psychologist can come by later and she might help me find answers."

Answers that terrified her.

"We can always cancel," Jake offered, reading her trepidation.

"But we shouldn't." She handed him the phone.

"Let's go back outside." He took her hand and led her into the gardens.

It was a gentle touch, not awkward or forced. Odd, she remembered something when he said the word *boyfriend,* but not this, not this natural, grounding touch.

"Besides going to church, nature also always makes me feel close to God," Jake said.

She wasn't sure about God, but being surrounded by the breathtaking colors of primrose, pansies and bluebells, eased the anxiety in her chest.

Jake turned to her. "Would you mind if we prayed for a minute?"

She shrugged.

He took both her hands in his and closed his eyes. "Dear Lord, we pray for strength to shoulder the challenges we will encounter in the next few days. We know through Your love and guidance we will choose the right path. Praise The Lord, Jesus Christ, Amen."

"Amen," she repeated.

He opened his eyes and searched Robin's. This man fascinated her with his faith and his tenderness, a man who'd served in war and most likely had taken lives in the service of his country.

"How do you do that?" she asked.

"What?" He let go of her hands, and she instantly missed the warmth.

"How do you find peace like that?" They walked back to the house, side by side, as if they were a couple.

"Jesus gives me peace, Robin. He gives us all peace. We just have to ask."

She puzzled over this, feeling like she either didn't deserve it, or Jesus simply didn't care enough about Robin to give her peace when she needed it most.

"Maybe you should try free association on me," he joked.

"Very funny. I've got you pretty much figured out."

They stepped onto the porch. "Yeah? I'm that much of a simpleton?"

She grabbed his arm. "No, I didn't mean—"

"I'm teasing."

"Oh." She smiled, and realized she was staring into his eyes, big time. She couldn't rip her gaze from this handsome face that gave her such strength. She felt a blush rising up her neck.

She snapped her eyes from his. "Let's keep going. Maybe we can figure this out before the woo-woo lady comes."

"Woo-woo?"

Robin shrugged. "Go ahead, ask me anything."

They settled into their chairs and she leaned back, a little less afraid. Was it the connection to Jesus that gave her strength? Or the support of this fine man?

"Movies," he said.

"Drive-in."

"Ice cream."

"Cone," she said

"Chocolate."

"Pretzels."

He smiled at that one. "Clouds?"

"Rain."

"Kyle."

"Dead."

EIGHT

Robin jumped out of her chair and paced the porch. "Dead? I know another dead man?" She fisted her hand and brought it to her mouth.

"Robin, calm down." Jake stood and she put out her hand to keep him at bay.

"Don't get too close," she said. "It could be dangerous. You could be killed, too."

"You don't know what it means. He could have died from natural causes."

She shot him a skeptical look.

"Let's not overreact about things until we know the truth." He motioned for her to sit down, but she couldn't.

The thought of being connected to yet another dead man sent her spinning in a new vortex of panic.

"How about some tea?" he suggested.

"Jake, we have to accept the possibility that I'm not one of the good guys."

"My instincts have never been wrong, and they're telling me you're a victim of circumstance. Nothing more."

A victim. The word made her angry. Well, angry was better than terrified, right?

"Come on, I'll make some tea," he offered.

"How's that supposed to help?" She regretted her tone but couldn't stop the frustration from rising up her throat.

"Tea always helped Mom." He opened the back door and she went into the kitchen, curious about his comment.

"Your mom was a victim like me?"

"You could say that." He filled the kettle with water and put it on the gas stove. He turned to her and leaned against the counter.

She read pain in his eyes and wanted to hug him. "I'm sorry," she said.

"It's okay."

"No, I should have left it alone."

"I've left it alone long enough. Doesn't do any good to ignore it. I know what it's like to hide from emotional trauma, pretend that everything's okay, that your home life is just like everyone else's."

She waited, didn't press him for more.

"Truth is, my dad wasn't a nice guy, couldn't control his temper. Mom took the brunt of it. She'd hide me and my sister in a closet, or up in the attic and tell us to wait until she said it was okay to come out."

"That must have been terrifying."

"Yeah, it was. I got out of the house as soon as I could, joined the army and left it all behind, or at least I thought I had."

"But you still think about it?"

"I do. I have regrets."

"Why? It's not your fault."

He pursed his lips and didn't respond. She wondered how he could blame himself for his father's abuse.

"What about your sister?" she said.

"She left a few years before me. I managed to stay away as much as possible. Then I went to boot camp and that was that."

Hardly. She could tell he was haunted by guilt.

"Water should be ready in a minute," he said, turning his back to her.

"Thanks, for sharing your story with a complete stranger."

"You're not a complete stranger. I know your favorite color and the fact you'd eat Market donuts for breakfast, lunch and dinner." He winked over his shoulder at her.

"I wish I didn't feel so alone, so detached from everything. It's like I don't exist." She fingered the lace tablecloth.

"I've got an idea." He opened a drawer and pulled out a tablet and pen.

"Not more free association games." She shuddered.

"Nope." He placed a legal pad and pen in front of her. "Go ahead and draw, whatever you want. Sometimes that frees up my brain when it's stuck."

"Thanks." He was being nice and she appreciated it, she really did, but she didn't want to think for a while, especially if it meant stirring up the frightening memories.

Coward.

No, she wasn't a coward. She was still bruised, both mentally and physically, and needed to rest and gain more strength to face what was ahead.

"Thanks for offering to make tea, but I think I'd like to lie down for a little while."

"Sure." He turned off the stove. "I can give you a hand upstairs, or…" He must have read her expression. She wanted to be independent, take care of herself.

"I can make it." She headed upstairs and sighed at the thought that when the psychologist arrived, she might come face-to-face with all her fears—not to mention, her true self.

She wanted to believe Jake, wanted to believe in his instincts that she was simply a victim, not a participant in the death of now two men.

She went to her room, shut the door and inhaled the scent of lilacs. A smile edged its way across her lips. She flopped down on the bed and remembered Jake's words:

Jesus gives me peace, Robin. He gives us all peace.

"Jesus, if you're listening…" she whispered and closed her eyes.

* * *

Two hours later Jake sat at the kitchen table surfing Sketch's extra laptop. Caroline had returned with clothes, hair color and essentials, but Jake's priority was finding out everything he could about Robin.

So he could better protect her.

Jake was pleasantly surprised by Sketch's IT set-up. The kid had enough equipment to stock a small computer store. It gave Jake the opportunity to do some research on the case and check email for information from Ethan.

He hesitated. What if someone was monitoring Jake's email account and could track the inn's IP address?

Sketch rushed through the kitchen, grabbing an apple and juice box from the fridge.

"Hey, kid, I've got a question for you," Jake said. "If I'm checking email from this computer and someone's monitoring my email, can they trace this IP address and find us?"

Sketch plopped down into a chair next to Jake. "On any normal computer they could." He grinned.

"But on this one…?" Jake encouraged.

"No one can trace anything on my computers. I've got a fire-wall the best hackers in the country couldn't break."

"Is that against the law, Sketch?" Caroline questioned, pulling ingredients from the refrigerator.

"It's not against the law to prevent people from looking into your personal accounts, Gran. Trust me. You'd be freaked to know how easy it is for someone to access your email accounts."

"Why would they want to?" Caroline said.

"No one will find you," Sketch said to Jake. "Oh, and I've got a Skype program set up so you can talk to someone and again, not have it traced to this IP address, in case you want a face-to-face with your detective friend."

"I owe you, kid."

"I'll collect." Sketch put his fist out, and Jake fist-bumped him. "Thanks."

"I gotta book."

"When are you—?" Caroline asked.

"Be back by five. Taking the bike for work on the brakes."

"Wear your helmet," Caroline said, but Sketch was already out the door.

She shook her head and shut the refrigerator door.

"Caroline?" Jake said.

She glanced at him.

"He's a good kid."

"Thanks." She leaned against the counter. "What happened with Rosalie?"

"I thought it better to cancel. Robin is exhausted, and the whole concept of hypnosis didn't sit well with her." He glanced at the second floor where she rested, he hoped peacefully.

"You like her."

He snapped his attention to Caroline, who was smiling at him.

"I'm protecting her," Jake clarified.

"Jake, honey, you can be honest with me."

"I've known her for less than three days."

"But in that time you've developed a connection—"

"Because she's in constant fear of being hurt. That's not a real relationship, Caroline."

"Maybe not, but neither was Cassandra."

"Here it comes," he muttered with a smile.

"I'm sorry, but that girl wasn't right for you."

"Maybe I wasn't right for her."

"Don't you dare take the blame for her self-absorbed, princess attitude."

"Did Mom know you felt this way?" he smiled.

"Of course, we talked about it all the time."

"She never talked to me about it."

"She loved you so much. She just wanted you to be happy. If Cassandra made you happy…"

"She did. For a while."

"But she wasn't the forever type. Now Robin, she's different."

"She can't remember a thing about her past. Once she does, I'm sure a boyfriend will be a part of the picture."

"We'll see." She winked and pulled out a mixing bowl. "God puts people in our lives for a reason."

Then why did Jake get stuck with an abusive father? Man, his emotions were hovering at the surface. Guess it was talking to Robin about his childhood, forming a bond of understanding with her that exposed his secrets. He rarely told people about Dad. He'd told Cassandra, and, in the end, she'd used it as a weapon against him.

"Your mother would be proud," Caroline whispered.

"Thanks, but too little, too late, on my part." He signed onto his email account, and felt Caroline's hand on his shoulder.

"Don't. She wouldn't want you blaming yourself. She'd want you to find a nice girl and have a family."

She was probably right, but Jake had given up on that fantasy. He wouldn't risk waking up one day and realizing he was just like the old man, that he would turn his resentment and rage on his own wife and children.

The front doorbell rang, and she slipped her hand off his shoulder. "Milk delivery," she said, whisking out of the kitchen.

Jake opened an email from Ethan and downloaded the attachment. The email itself was blank, and Jake figured Ethan didn't want to expose his thoughts about the case.

With a deep breath, Jake opened the document and scanned the contents.

Robin Strand, 29, special events coordinator for Anna Marsh Pediatric Cancer Foundation, lives in Greenlake area of Seattle, attends an aerobics class twice a week. He scanned the PDF document for background. *Attended Washington University. Grew up in Seattle. One sibling, an older brother, Kyle.*

Deceased at age 14.

He glanced at the ceiling. "How am I going to tell you that, sweetheart?"

Better question: should he? Maybe that's why her distant memories were as blocked as recent ones, because she'd never fully healed from the trauma of losing her brother.

Jake knew that victims of post-traumatic stress should remember on their own and not be forced into remembering the trauma. Yet he and Robin didn't have the luxury of time. Jake felt relatively safe at the inn, but they couldn't hide out here forever.

Although a part of him wanted to.

"Snap out of it." This was no time for dreaming of things he could never have. Robin was in trouble and needed him to think straight and be objective, not let his emotions pull him away from reality.

The reality was he'd do whatever was necessary to help Robin remember and protect her from a killer.

Maybe, then, Jake would finally feel some sort of redemption.

A few hours later, Robin came downstairs. She hadn't slept exactly. No, it was more like she'd fought a wrestling match with one side of her brain struggling to remember, while the other side put up wall after wall, blocking her from any clear recall.

What was she so afraid of? She'd remembered flashes of the shooting and survived the memory. What more could there be? Besides, she was safe at the inn with Jake as her bodyguard.

She wished his desire to help her was by choice, not by fate. It was fate he happened to be standing outside the building—a good thing, sure, but it also saddened her. The only person who cared about her was here out of duty. She could be anybody in trouble, and Jake would be protecting her.

"Now what are you thinking about?" she whispered to herself.

She padded down the hallway to the kitchen, the gathering place. As she passed a mirror in the hallway she caught her reflection. Half-moon circles shadowed under her eyes, but otherwise she looked pretty good for a woman whose life was in jeopardy.

As she approached the kitchen, she hesitated at the sound of Jake's voice.

"It would destroy her. I can't risk it."

Fingertips on the door, she took a slow, deep breath. Was he talking about her?

"I understand that, Ethan, but you're going to have to trust that I know what I'm doing when it comes to post-traumatic situations. She'll remember when she's ready."

A few seconds passed.

"I'm sorry. I know he was a good man."

"Robin? Can I get you something?" Caroline said, coming downstairs and spotting her outside the kitchen.

"No, I—"

The kitchen door swung open and, holding a phone to his ear, Jake eyed Robin. "I've gotta go."

Jake motioned her into the kitchen. When she didn't move at first, he said, "How much did you hear?"

"Enough."

"Then let's talk." He glanced over her shoulder at Caroline. "Can we have the kitchen for a few minutes?"

"Of course."

Robin went into the kitchen and glanced out the window overlooking the gardens. "What is it?"

"Do you trust me?" he said.

She spun around to face him. "Do I have a choice?"

"You always have a choice. Do you trust that I want to protect you?"

"Yes."

"Then let me keep doing that, okay?"

"You're keeping something from me."

He shifted into a kitchen chair. She suspected he wanted to give her the illusion of power over this conversation. "I learned some things about you, but I'd rather you remember them on your own."

"I'm not." She hesitated and, in her head, heard a female voice *Be a good girl*.

"I'm not a criminal or something, am I?"

"No, of course not."

"What, then?"

He hesitated and glanced at the laptop on the kitchen table as if he wanted to say more. "You grew up in Queen Anne. I found a picture of your childhood home if you want to see it."

Fear kept her glued to the counter. What would she remember if she looked at the house?

"Who died?" she asked.

"You remember?" he said, hopeful. He leaned forward in his chair.

"I heard you talking on the phone. You said, 'he was a good man.'"

Jake glanced at the floor. "Right, that." With each passing second her heartbeat sped a little faster.

"Jake?"

Regret colored his blue-green eyes. "Detective Monroe died an hour ago."

The room tipped sideways and she turned to grip the counter for support.

"Hey, hey," Jake said, standing and coming up beside her. With firm hands on her shoulders, Jake pulled her against his chest. "Take a deep breath. It's okay."

Rage bubbled up in her chest. She wrenched free of him and paced to the back door. "It's not okay. I can't breathe."

She flung open the door and raced toward the beautiful gardens, the one place that offered her peace. What was going on? She didn't even know Detective Monroe that well.

Still, he was dead. Because of her.

"Robin," Jake called. She couldn't turn around, ashamed to look into his eyes.

"Why me? Why did I get to live, and he didn't?" She gasped at the words, remembering something so tragic, so devastating, that it squeezed her heart.

"It's unfortunate, but it was his job," Jake said. "He knew the risk when he joined the force."

"That's not good enough." She turned to him. "It's so random, me being at the office, seeing a man get shot. Why did I have to be there at that very moment? Why have two detectives been killed, yet I lived? What's so special about me?"

"Come here." He pulled her against his chest.

A choke-sob escaped her lips as she wrapped her arms around his waist.

"Things just happen," he said. "It's not your fault."

But it felt like her fault, her fault that she was in the wrong place at the wrong time, that Detective Monroe was dead, and that she was so helpless.

She hated the feeling and refused to let it consume her any longer.

"I'm done," she said, breaking the embrace.

"Excuse me?"

"I'm done being afraid. I need to remember what happened last night. Maybe if I call Jenn… I was talking to her when I witnessed the shooting."

"You sure?"

"Yes, unless you think they'll trace the call."

"No, Sketch figured out a way to avoid that."

"I had her number but lost it at the safe house."

"Not a problem."

They went into the house. Jake opened a file on the laptop, scribbled down a number and handed it to Robin.

"Where did you find it?" she said.

"Ethan sent over a complete background check on you this morning, including friends and emergency contacts."

Talk about exposed. Robin sighed at the thought Jake knew more about her than she did.

Using Sketch's phone, Robin dialed Jenn's number and waited. It rang two, three times. She took a deep breath and stood a few feet away from Jake. She had to stop relying on him so much. His motivation was protecting her because he'd made a promise. Once the case was resolved, he'd be gone.

Just like everyone else in her life.

She leaned against the counter. Everyone else in her life?

"Hello?" Jenn answered.

"Jenn, it's Robin."

A pause, then, "Where are you? You just disappeared, and the police are looking for you, and I thought the bad guy got you, and I called your apartment, but no one answered and—"

"Stop. It's okay. I'm fine." She glanced at Jake. "Look, I can't talk long. I need you to tell me exactly what you heard last night when we were talking on the phone." Robin sat at the kitchen table across from Jake.

"Okay, sure. Well, you were at work, at nine on a Friday night," she said. "You really shouldn't have been there, Robin."

"I work too much, I know. Continue." Robin closed her eyes and took a deep, calming breath.

"I tried getting you out of there with the promise of a longhorn burger and time with Trent. Anyway, I think you'd locked up and were on your way to the elevator when I heard a loud bang."

"What did I say right before the line went dead?"

"I think you said, 'he shot him'? Then, nothing."

Robin hyper-focused on replaying the scene in her head, but nothing came. With a frustrated sigh, she stood and paced into the front hallway. What made her think talking with Jenn would somehow jog her memory?

"Robin?" Jenn said. "Please tell me where you are. I can come get you."

"No, it's too dangerous."

"At least tell me you're safe, and in a nice place, not some dump. I hate to think of you being stuck in some—"

"Don't worry. We're at a lovely inn. It's safe. Listen, I'd better go."

"When are you coming back?"

"I'm not sure. Take care." Robin wandered back into the kitchen and sat at the table across from Jake.

"You okay?" he asked.

"Who am I kidding?"

"You didn't remember anything?"

"Zippo."

"Don't rush it," he said. "It will come back to you."

"What if it doesn't? I mean, ever?" She eyed him, wondering what hospital he'd commit her to.

The back door burst open and Sketch rushed into the kitchen and straight for the sink. "Where's Gran?"

He flipped on the water and leaned over the basin. Robin noted his disheveled appearance, muddy jeans and torn T-shirt.

"Upstairs doing book work I think, why?" Jake asked.

"Good. If she sees me like this, I'm toast."

"What happened?" Jake pushed.

"I ruined the one decent shirt she bought me, that's what." Sketch turned around and Robin gasped at the sight of blood covering his shirt.

"Kid, you okay?" Jake said, but his voice sounded far away.

Robin couldn't take her eyes off the bright red, spreading across his shirt....

A memory shot across her mind. A crisp white shirt covered in blood...spreading across the industrial carpeting.

Then she looked up—up into the eyes of a killer.

"I can see his face," she whispered and looked at Jake. "I can see Death Eyes's face."

NINE

Jake wasn't sure what to do first, tend to the kid's injury or help Robin. It looked like she was about to pass out.

Jake kneeled beside her and touched her bare arm. "Robin?"

"I'm okay. Take care of Sketch."

"You sure?"

"Yes."

Jake went to Sketch, who grimaced in pain. "Ruining the shirt looks like the least of your problems. Let me see."

Sketch jutted out his chin. "I'm fine."

"As in, 'I need a butterfly bandage' fine, or 'get me to the medical clinic' fine? I won't know until I get a look at it."

Sketch hesitated, and Jake motioned to see Sketch's arm. "What happened?"

"Fell off my bike."

"You were wearing a helmet, I hope."

"Not that it helped my arm." Clenching his jaw, Sketch extended his forearm, and Jake examined it, a two-inch gash, not too deep.

"I don't think you'll need stitches," Jake said. "Where does your grandmother keep the first aid kit?"

"Why, who's hurt?" Caroline said, stepping into the kitchen. Her eyes caught sight of Sketch. "My word, what happened?"

"I fell off my bike, no big deal."

Caroline rushed over and practically shouldered Jake out of the way, so she could tend to her grandson. That was always her style, hover and nurture until the patient felt better. Mom always felt better after a visit to the inn. She'd return home with renewed strength and determination to put an end to her husband's abuse.

But once Caroline's magic touch wore off, Mom would slip back into traumatized-victim mode.

Jake glanced at Robin. She seemed fascinated by Caroline's nurturing touch.

"Sorry," Sketch said to his grandmother.

"For what? Accidents happen." She cleaned his wound with a wet washcloth.

"I ruined the shirt," Sketch said.

Caroline applied a gauze bandage. "You didn't like that shirt anyway." She smiled and brushed his bangs out of his eyes.

The touch was gentle and loving, and Jake had a flashback about falling out of a neighbor's tree house and Mom taking care of him afterward.

The guilt started low in his gut, guilt that he had been unable to return the favor. Which was one of the reasons he was driven to protect Robin.

And the best way to protect her was to take the offense. She had just remembered the shooter's face. It was a breakthrough. He wondered what else she remembered.

"I should call Ethan. He'll probably want you to meet with a sketch artist," Jake said to Robin. "And I'd better change my looks before we venture out in public."

"Hair color and freshly washed clothes are upstairs in your room," Caroline offered. "I put Robin's clothes in your room, Jake, because she was resting, and I didn't want to disturb her."

"Thanks." Robin went to Caroline and gave her a hug. "I really appreciate everything you've done."

"My pleasure."

They broke the embrace, and Caroline shot a questioning look at Jake. He wondered what Robin's relationship was like with her mother. She seemed to bask in the attention from Caroline. But then, Caroline was a loving, positive woman who could warm even the coldest of hearts.

"I'd better go do my hair," Jake said. "I can't believe I just said that."

"I'd like to help with something to keep my mind off things," Robin said to Caroline.

"You can help me set up for afternoon tea," Caroline offered.

"You sure you're up to it?" Jake asked. After all, she'd just remembered a traumatic image.

"It will keep my brain occupied," Robin said.

"Where's Mack?" Sketch asked.

"At the Rubins', down the street."

"As in Ashley Rubin?" Sketch said.

"Yes, she's watching him for me, why?"

Sketch shrugged. "I'll be downstairs."

"Take the shirt off so you don't get blood everywhere, please," Caroline ordered.

"Yes, ma'am."

"Sketch, can I use the Batphone again?" Jake asked.

The kid smiled, liking the reference to the comic book hero. "Sure." He ran into the basement and brought the phone back to Jake.

"I'll be on the porch calling Ethan." As he placed his hand on the screen door, he hesitated and glanced over his shoulder at the women. They worked together fluidly, Caroline giving orders in a firm, but soft, voice, telling Robin where to find the linen napkins, the china cups, the sugar and creamer.

He wondered if this was what a loving home looked like, a mother and daughter bonding over putting out a spread for family or, in this case, guests.

Jake had missed that growing up. He'd missed feeling safe

and loved as they sat down to dinner because they had been too worried about avoiding the violence.

"Jake, honey?" Caroline said.

He realized Robin and Caroline were staring at him.

"You okay?" Robin asked.

"Yeah, just…" What? Realizing what he'd missed growing up and would never have? "I'll be outside."

Robin sensed Jake's tension as they drove to the ferry to meet up with the sketch artist. Detective Beck said he'd found an artist he'd worked with before, someone he could trust to keep quiet about this assignment.

Still, from Jake's body language, Robin knew he was in defensive mode, so unlike his posture back at the inn. He fit in surprisingly well there, with Caroline, Sketch and even the little boy, Mack. Robin found it hard to believe someone like Jake wasn't married with children of his own, but he'd been a military man, then a government agent, and, most recently, a caregiver for his mom. Still, a busy life was no reason to be single, right?

Yet, Robin was single. Jenn said Robin was interested in Trevor, which must mean Robin didn't have a serious boyfriend or fiancé. Anxiety clawed its way up from her subconscious.

No, with her memories came determination to take back her life and fight for what she wanted. Personal safety topped that list.

"So, what's the plan once we get there?" she asked.

"You hang back. I'll meet the artist at the ferry dock," Jake said.

"How will you know him?"

"He'll be wearing a Chicago White Sox baseball cap."

She glanced at him in question.

"Ethan used to be a big Chicago sports fan. His uncle lives on the South Side."

"Do you think someone will follow the artist onto the ferry?"

"Unlikely, but we should be ready for anything."

They found street parking and Jake scanned the surrounding shops and restaurants before motioning for Robin to get out of the car. He'd driven Caroline's vintage Chevy, so they wouldn't be identified by his truck.

As she shut the car door, she caught a glimpse of her reflection in the window. She was unrecognizable, even to herself, with her blond, cropped hair, glasses and pale blue sundress and white sweater. Jake wore a pressed shirt, tie and navy suit jacket over jeans.

She remembered the clothes she'd been wearing when she was brought into the hospital: simple, professional and boring. At least her sundress and sweater had a little style to it.

Walking side by side, Jake and Robin looked like a romantic couple on an evening out. She almost took his hand to complete the picture but caught herself.

"What?" he said, glancing sideways at her.

"Nothing." She smiled.

"It will be okay."

He took her hand and gave it a squeeze. They approached the crosswalk, and she spotted a lighthouse in the distance, a beacon of hope. She hesitated and glanced up into Jake's blue-green eyes, wishing, just for a second, that they were a real couple, not two people thrown together by violence.

"Robin?" he said in such a soft voice she wasn't sure he'd spoken.

They paused. With a tender smile, he reached out and slipped a few strands of hair behind her ear. She closed her eyes, leaning into his touch.

Everything fell away, as she drifted into a moment of sincere and utter peace. Was this what love felt like?

He slipped his hand from her cheek, and she sighed, missing his warmth. She opened her eyes and caught him frowning as he glanced across the street at the ferry dock.

"What's wrong?" She followed his gaze. The ferry was still off in the distance, the glow reflecting off the water.

"I shouldn't have touched you like that," he said.

"Why not?" She studied him.

"In these types of highly charged situations, people can get confused about things."

"Meaning?"

He pinned her with serious eyes. "They can develop feelings for one another that are not real."

"Define real."

"Look, we've known each other a short time and I sense you, well…"

"You sense I like you?"

"Yes."

"What's wrong with that?"

"You hardly know me."

"I know enough."

"It's too intense for the short amount of time we've known each other."

"Haven't you ever heard of love at first sight?" She regretted the words the minute they left her lips. She sounded like a silly kid with a schoolgirl crush.

"Of course, but we're not teenagers, and I think this is really about—"

"What? That transference thing?" she interrupted.

"Pretty much."

"So, it can't possibly be that I like you because you're a nice guy, a good man with a sense of humor and a calming force in my life? It's got to be that other thing, right?"

He glanced down but didn't answer.

"You believe in God. Why can't you have a little faith in what we're feeling for each other?"

He kept silent and frustration welled up in her chest.

"Whatever." She crossed the street, wrapping her sweater tighter around her to ward off the night chill.

Am I wrong, God? Is my brain so messed up that I'm falling for a guy because he's convenient?

Logically, it may not make sense, but she knew in her heart there was more to this relationship.

"Robin," he called after her.

She kept walking, found a quiet spot by the wooden fence and leaned against it, watching the lights of the ferry reflect off Puget Sound.

Jake stepped up beside her. "I didn't mean to upset you."

"It's okay." She glanced up at him. "We should be focused on the case. What happens after the sketch artist draws the picture?"

"He'll take it back to Ethan, who will use it to track down the perp."

"When will we go back?"

"When Ethan says it's safe. He feels responsible for the deaths of two police officers, so he's determined to solve this thing quickly."

"I hope so."

A few minutes passed. Muted music echoed from a restaurant behind them. The ferry approached the dock.

"You didn't remember anything other than the shooter's face?" Jake asked.

"Like what?"

"I don't know." He glanced at the ferry as it docked. "Like, anything about your family or work or where you went to school?"

"No, sorry."

"Don't be sorry." He rubbed her shoulder and offered a charming smile. "I'm going to meet the artist. You stay back, out of sight." He handed her the car keys. "If you see anything odd or dangerous, take off."

She took the keys, but had no intention of leaving without him.

As he walked away from her, he ran two fingers between his

shirt collar and neck, obviously uncomfortable in the restrictive clothes. He started up the ramp and she found a spot behind a cluster of bushes where she could see through the foliage yet was sufficiently hidden.

She kept her eyes trained on Jake as he paced the walkway waiting for the artist. There weren't a ton of passengers disembarking this late at night, so it shouldn't be hard to spot him.

Robin watched cars pull off the ferry, and a few walk-ons passed by her on the other side of the bushes. A good ten minutes later, the ferry had seemingly emptied. Jake planted his hands on his hips and glanced back at where Robin had been standing. He squinted into the darkness as if concerned. Just as she was about to step out and let him know she was okay, two men blocked her view as they passed. She recognized one of them.

Death Eyes.

She stifled a gasp and whipped her gaze back to Jake. He was coming her way, and he had no idea of the danger standing just feet from her.

"Robin?" Jake called out, concerned because he couldn't see her.

Before she could warn him, the two men closed in. Jake had nowhere to run. They said something—Robin couldn't hear what—and cornered Jake against the fence bordering the water.

She wouldn't allow another person to die because of her, especially not Jake. She was alive thanks to him, and she planned to keep on living.

She had so much to do, projects to complete.

She had to make Kyle proud.

Make your brother proud.

Sadness flooded her chest as she watched Jake. Death Eyes's partner, a short, stocky man, grabbed Jake's arms and held them behind his back. Death Eyes fisted his hand and slugged Jake in the stomach.

Robin gritted her teeth. "No."

She snapped her gaze to the crowded restaurant behind her. A plan unfolded in her head. With determination rushing through her body, she stepped out from behind the bushes. "Hey! You guys looking for me?"

TEN

Death Eyes shoved Jake against the fence and looked over, squinting at Robin. He said something over his shoulder to his partner, who kicked Jake in the stomach and tossed him over the fence into the water.

No! Her bold move was supposed to distract them from beating Jake up. Panic blinded her for a second, then adrenaline kicked in when she realized they were marching toward her.

It was a good plan turned disastrous if Jake didn't survive. She rushed into The Wild Grill Restaurant on the corner, through the crowded dining room where people clapped their hands and sang along to the live country band.

She had to get back to Jake, save him. Yeah, how was she going to do that? He was the military man, the warrior, and he couldn't defend himself against the men.

She may not have the physical strength, but she had the mental intelligence to think her way out of this.

Never as smart as your brother...

"Shut up," she muttered, shaking off the voices of her past.

Making her way to the ladies' room, she shucked her sweater and tied it around her waist to slightly change her appearance. A few ladies smiled as they passed her coming out of the bathroom.

And that's when she spotted it in the hallway: the fire alarm.

Thank You, Lord.

She glanced down the empty hallway. Took a deep breath. She pulled the alarm and ducked back into the bathroom. Once she heard people being herded down the hall, she'd jump out and escape with the flow of patrons.

Standing behind the door, she waited, listening to the sounds of panic. She readied herself to jump out into the crowd.

The bathroom door cracked open, and the stocky guy reflected back at her in the mirror. She held her breath. Waited.

No place to go. Cornered. It was loud in the hallway and no one would hear her if she called out for help.

"Hey, everybody out," a male voice said to the stocky guy.

"But my wife—"

"I'm sure she's out by now. Come on."

The door slammed shut. "Uh," Robin breathed, gripping her sundress's bodice.

There was no time to waste. She had to get to Jake. She whipped open the door and stepped into the hallway. She made eye contact with an older woman with gold star earrings and a warm smile. The woman motioned for Robin to walk ahead of her, and Robin smiled her thanks.

The parking lot filled with patrons who hovered, eyeing the restaurant apparently trying to figure out where the fire would pop up. Sirens echoed down the street as a fire engine, an ambulance, and a few squad cars pulled in front of the restaurant.

Robin scanned the crowd looking for Death Eyes.

Stop thinking about him and focus on Jake. How to get to him. How to save him.

The older woman gathered with a group in the parking lot. They speculated on what started the fire.

"I need to get home, anyway," one of the women said.

"It could be hours before they let us back in," another offered.

If Robin stayed close enough, it would look like she was part of their group.

"Hey, so does this happen often?" she asked, stepping up beside star-earring lady.

"Not in months. They had problems with the computer circuits or something earlier in the year."

"Bad wiring, I heard," another lady said.

"Probably kids trying to be funny," a third offered.

As the women discussed what caused the fire alarm, Robin eyed the restaurant and spotted Death Eyes and his partner headed around the front of the building in the opposite direction. *Nice!*

"Well, see you later," Robin said to the women.

"You need a ride somewhere?" the lady with the star earrings offered.

"No, I'm good, thanks."

And she would be, as soon as she found Jake. That was assuming he was still alive.

She quickly headed toward the water. "I won't accept any other possibility."

Moonlight glittered off the water as she climbed down to the rocky beach. They'd tossed Jake over the railing about twenty feet from shore. She shielded herself from view beneath the pier, took off her shoes and stepped into the water. Boats of every shape and size lined the nearby slip, and, for half a second she considered escaping in one of them, but she knew nothing about boats. At least, she didn't think she did… No, she'd have to get Jake back to the car.

If she found him.

Determination drove her deeper into the water, which now reached midcalf. "Jake?" she whispered.

Soft waves crawled across the rocky shore and receded back into Puget Sound. A few feet away, on the other side of a wooden pylon, she spotted something on the shore. Her heart dropped to her feet.

A body.

Jake's body.

"No, no, no." She scanned the area, then waded back to the shore. She stumbled as she got closer and kneeled beside him. Biting back the pain from her sore knee, she placed her hand on Jake's back.

"Jake?" she said. "Come on, we've gotta go."

He was so cold and still. So…dead?

No, she wouldn't allow it. She fought back the panic.

"Get up." She gently rolled him onto his side and caught sight of blood oozing from his lip.

Blinking a few times, he opened his eyes. "What…what are you doing?" he said.

"We are getting out of here. Come on, get up."

With a moan, he got to his knees, and she helped him stand with his arm around her shoulder.

"What happened?"

"Death Eyes and his partner tossed you into the water."

"I mean…" He stopped and leaned against a pylon. "What did you do? You called out to them? Why?"

"I had to get them away from you. Come on." She slipped on her shoes and reached for his arm, but he jerked back.

"Don't you ever do that again," he said, his body trembling from being dunked in the frigid water.

"Let's argue later," she said. "We've got to get away. Let's go."

"They're up there waiting for us."

"I'm sure they are, but the streets are packed with people right now, plus emergency crews, so there's a lot going on to distract them."

"What—"

"Can you please stop with the questions? I want to get back to the inn."

He didn't budge, his eyes clouded with confusion. Sure he was confused. *She* was saving *him* for a change.

Figuring he was a little out of it from being beaten and tossed into frigid water, she tried another tact.

"Jake, I'm freezing." She fingered the wet hem of her dress. The material was soaked to just above her knees. "Come on, please?"

She knew he'd be more likely to move to make her comfortable than to take care of himself.

With a nod, he stepped toward her and she put his arm around her shoulder to help him balance. They climbed up the shore to the walkway, Robin cataloging every person outside the restaurant, hoping to catch sight of their pursuers, so she could avoid them.

"Robin." Jake hesitated. "You need to make me a promise."

"What's that?" She encouraged him to pick up his pace. She knew he had to be stiff and freezing, but they had to get to the car before Death Eyes spotted them.

"Promise me you'll never do that again," he said.

"What? Go swimming in my dress?" she joked. She suspected where he was going.

"Put yourself in danger for me. Promise me."

"I'm sorry, Jake. I can't do that."

They were only half a block away from the car. Luckily, it was parked far enough away from the restaurant to make a quiet and safe escape, if they weren't noticed.

A group of patrons blocked the sidewalk ahead.

"Excuse us," Robin said. One of the guys, early twenties, spotted Jake's wet clothes and bloody lip.

"Whoa, dude, what happened to you?" he said.

Drat. Just what they didn't need was to draw attention to themselves. Out of the corner of her eye, she spotted someone plowing through the group and feared it was Death Eyes. She wouldn't look back, wouldn't let him intimidate her into giving up. She knew he wouldn't make an overtly violent move in public. He'd wait until they were closer to the car.

She remembered the moves Jake had taught her. She calmed her breathing and readied for whatever might happen next. As she clung to Jake for support, she realized he was wavering, as if he was losing strength. Was he going to pass out?

They were so close to the car she could reach out and touch the shiny hood.

Suddenly, someone grabbed Jake and shoved him chest first into the hood of the car. Not Death Eyes, but his stocky partner.

"Robin, get outta here!" Jake ordered as Stocky Guy punched him in the lower back. Jake grunted and struggled to get free, but he was pinned, freezing and probably about to pass out.

"Hey!" she shouted at the guy. "Leave him alone."

Stocky Guy turned, a creepy grin curling his lips. "And if I don't? What are you gonna do?"

"What am I going to do? I'm going to pray."

He burst out laughing, which is what she'd hoped for. Just as Jake had taught her, she fired off the palm heel strike—one, two three—to his nose and his ribs. He doubled over and fell to his knees.

"Come on." She led Jake to the front seat, slammed the door and zipped around the car to get behind the wheel. A few bystanders wandered up to the stocky guy to inquire about his condition. Good, they'd block his view of the license plate as she drove off.

She shoved the car in gear and hit the accelerator but kept to the speed limit. Eyes darting from the road to the rearview mirror, she focused on calming the adrenaline rush that could surely cloud her thinking. She couldn't afford that right now. Not with her and Jake's lives on the line.

Another squad car sped past them toward the scene of the fire alarm. Holding the steering wheel with more force than necessary, she realized clutching the wheel helped her fight back the panic that she'd been denying since she'd first spotted the thugs.

The scene replayed itself in her head: the two men beating up Jake and tossing him into the water, Death Eyes chasing her, setting off the fire alarm, escaping the restaurant and finding Jake in the water, unconscious.

She thought she might have lost him for good. Anxiety ripped through her body at the thought. Yet she'd only known him a short time. Didn't matter. Jake Walters was the center of her life right now, and she wouldn't let anything happen to him.

Jake moaned and gripped his side.

"Jake? Hey, you okay?" She glanced in the rearview mirror to make sure they weren't being followed.

"I'm alive." He clenched his jaw and sat up. "Thanks to the Karate Kid."

"I had a good teacher."

"I'd have to disagree with that."

"Why, was my form off?" she quipped, trying to ease the tension.

"Your form was fine. But obviously I didn't teach you how to take orders." He narrowed his eyes. "I told you not to put yourself in danger for me."

"How are your ribs?"

"What?"

"Didn't he slug you in the ribs?" she pressed.

"Don't change the subject."

"I'm trying to decide if we should find an emergency clinic or—"

"No, head back to the inn." He glanced at the side mirror. "Is anyone following us?"

"Doesn't look like it."

"But if they got the plate number, it won't take them long to find us."

"I don't think he did. The guy was pretty out of it, then a crowd gathered."

"Bragging, are you?" he teased.

"Man, you're feisty."

"Sorry, trying to keep my mind off my body."

She eyed him. "You're hurt bad, aren't you?"

"Not too bad," he grunted. "You remember the way home?"

Home. Odd, but the inn felt like home, and they'd only been there a day.

"Yes."

"Good. I need to zone out for a minute." He leaned back against the seat and closed his eyes. Robin refocused on getting them back to the inn safely, without further incident.

Even in the dark car, she could see his body trembling from the chill of being dunked in the water. She wouldn't risk hypothermia. They had a three-hour drive back to Port Whisper, and he was stuck in soggy clothes.

She turned on the heater and then clicked on the radio, setting it on low to a soft rock station. She had to warm up Jake, and she wouldn't wait until they got back home.

It was a slip of his tongue, yet she liked him referring to the inn as home. She also liked the thought of taking long drives with Jake, not trembling of course, hiking the Olympic Mountains, maybe even seeing a movie.

What was the matter with her, daydreaming about something that probably wasn't meant to be? She decided it was okay to dream if it kept her focused on the one thing she'd lost since the accident: hope.

"I left her at a safe house," Jake grunted against the bruised ribs.

"That's a lie," the tall guy with the black eyes said. *Cold, soulless eyes.*

He must be Death Eyes, Jake thought.

"We know how attached the woman is to you," he paused. *"We're going to use her feelings for you to get her back."* He smiled. *"And kill her. After we do a thorough interrogation..."*

Get away, Robin. Run.

"Hey, you looking for me?" she cried out.

Jake gasped and sat up, struggling to breathe.

"Jake, it's okay. You're okay," her sweet voice said.

Chest heaving as he fought off the nightmare, he glanced around to figure out where he was. The car was dark, but they weren't moving. They were parked in a secluded area behind a public park.

"Where...where are we?"

"I pulled over to see if we were being followed. I thought we should call Caroline to find out if anyone has been looking for us."

He studied her, hearing the killer's voice in his head.

We're going to use her feelings for you to get her back...and kill her.

Jake collapsed against the seat and realized their pursuers had the best weapon they could use against Jake: knowledge of the enemy. They knew something was developing between Jake and Robin, because she completely depended on Jake. It was a quick and natural transference. Any idiot could figure that out.

Robin was developing feelings for Jake, and the truth was, it would be way too easy for Jake to return the feelings.

"Are you...angry with me?" she asked.

He glanced out the passenger window. "No." He was angry with the situation, angry that they'd met this way, that whatever developed between them in the next few days was a mirage, an illusion.

As he turned to face her, he noticed he was covered with blankets. "Where did you get these?"

"Sanders General Store. I stopped for supplies a few hours back," she explained.

Jake stiffened. "You stopped and got out of the car and...what did you use for money?"

She nibbled her lower lip. "I kinda borrowed your wallet, but I figured you'd do the same for me if I was suffering from hypothermia."

"I was suffering from... You what?" he said.

"See you're confused. That's definitely a sign of hypothermia."

He didn't how to respond to that one. Maybe she was right, maybe he was suffering from hypothermia. But that was irrelevant.

"I feel like a broken record," he muttered.

"Why? What hurts?" she reached over to adjust the blankets.

"Stop." He grabbed her wrist, but her hand had already landed on his chest. The touch pierced through the layers of blankets, making his heart ache.

It struck him that his mother's touch had always been one of panic as she'd shuffled him off to one hiding place or another. It had never felt like this, calming and nurturing.

Man, he was losing it.

"Let's say you're right, that I'm a little foggy," he started. "That means, just for now, you have to think for me, too. And think smart, okay?"

"Sure."

He wished she'd move her hand. The pressure above his heart was crushing him with something he couldn't name. He slid her hand off his chest.

"Our goal is to keep you alive so you can identify the shooter and get your life back, right?"

"And to get my memories back."

"None of that's going to happen if they—" he hesitated and decided this was time for harsh reality "—if they find you and kill you."

"They won't. You promised to protect me."

"Robin, I can't protect you if you put yourself in danger over and over again."

"I wasn't—"

"You offered yourself up to them at the ferry landing."

"I had a plan."

"You stopped for blankets, exposing yourself to who-knows-what."

"I had to help you."

"No. No, you don't. I can take care of myself."

I can take care of myself, Mommy. Fight back. Don't let him hit you anymore.

He suddenly let go of her wrist and leaned away. His thoughts, his emotions were all over the place, and, in this shape, he was no good to anybody.

"We should call the inn to see if it's safe to return," he said, glancing out the passenger window. "Let's find a pay phone."

"Jake?"

He didn't answer, didn't look at her. Panic rushed through his body, more powerful than the adrenaline rush of pursuing insurgents, worse than the rush of being shot at.

"I wish you'd talk to me," she said.

But he couldn't utter a word for fear the wrong words would come out, something like, *Why don't you listen to me? Do you enjoy the abuse?*

"I'll find a pay phone." She pulled out of the parking lot and headed north.

They drove a solid fifteen minutes in silence. Jake's brain drifted from anger to exhaustion to panic. She was right, he was suffering from moderate hypothermia, and he needed to raise his body temperature. The blankets helped, but weren't able to do the trick against the wet clothes soaking his skin.

In this shape he was as useless as…

As a child trying to protect his mother against a monster.

"There's a pay phone," she said, interrupting Jake's internal rantings.

She pulled into a gas station and parked beside a public phone. "What's the number?" she said.

"I'll do it." He opened the car door and clenched his jaw as he stepped onto the asphalt. Before he could say conspiracy, she was beside him, helping him stand.

"We'll do it," she said in a firm tone.

"Here, Sketch's private number." He pulled a soggy scrap of

paper out of his pocket. She unfolded it carefully and made the collect call, then handed Jake the phone.

"Yeah, what's up?" Sketch said.

"We ran into a little trouble," Jake said. "Has anyone called the inn looking for us?"

"Phone hasn't rung all night. How would they find you?"

"License plate."

"You drove the Impala?"

"Yeah." He gripped his bruised ribs.

"No problem. I think that car's still registered in Gramps's business name. It's got a Sequim address."

Jake exhaled with relief. They'd caught a break. The killer wouldn't track them from the license plate. They were safe—for now.

"Hey, you there?" Sketch said.

Jake grew lightheaded and handed Robin the phone. "I gotta sit." Jake inched back to the car.

"Thanks, Sketch. Gotta go," she said.

Jake had to ground himself or he was going to faint like a wimp, like a…

Worthless little brat, hiding behind a woman. Stand up for yourself, fight back.

"You're okay," Robin said, helping him into the car.

"Have to stay awake," he said. She needed him to protect her, defend her from the men who were sure to find them. The men…

We're going to use her feelings for you to get her back…and kill her.

As he fought for consciousness, his last thought was that he'd failed…

Again.

ELEVEN

They made it back to the inn where Caroline was waiting with reinforcements. Sketch and Police Chief Wright got Jake into dry clothes, Caroline found an electric blanket, and Robin tucked it firmly around his body.

Luckily, Chief Wright was a close friend of a doctor who didn't hesitate coming over at the late hour to check on Jake. While he did the exam, Robin told the police chief what had happened: the missing sketch artist, the attack and escape.

That was six hours ago. After the doctor had assured everyone Jake would be fine given rest and liquids, the chief and the doctor left, and Caroline went to sleep.

But not Robin. She pulled up a chair beside Jake's bed and held his hand, wanting him to know, in whatever unconscious state he was in, that it was going to be okay.

The doctor's words haunted her: he's a tough cookie, just like his mom.

Robin grew angry at the thought of Jake as a little boy being tormented by a brutal father. How could his mother let that happen? And what scars did that leave on Jake's psyche?

One thing for sure, he didn't like Robin putting herself in danger for him. It was starting to make sense. He probably spent his life trying to earn redemption because he couldn't protect his mom.

Now he'd promised to protect Robin and probably thought he'd failed last night when the thugs got the jump on him. That puzzled her. Jake was a strong and cunning warrior. He might have been outnumbered, but she sensed something else had weakened him in the split second before the thugs got the advantage.

But she had gotten it back, determined not to be responsible for Jake being hurt—or killed.

She jumped up and paced to the window. As she watched the early morning sun light the town of Port Whisper, she questioned why she had this kind of visceral reaction to losing a man who was a virtual stranger.

"Robin? Honey?" Caroline said.

Robin glanced at the doorway where Caroline stood, flanked by Sketch and little Mack.

"Hey," she said.

"You never came down for breakfast."

"I wasn't hungry."

"How's he doing?"

"Still asleep," Robin said. "He hasn't had much sleep in the last few days so maybe he's making up for it."

Caroline shooed the boys away and came into the room, adjusting Jake's blankets and placing the back of her hand to his forehead.

Robin stilled at a sudden rush of memory. She'd seen this before, her own mother feeling for a fever, tucking in...

Kyle. Her legs weakened and she collapsed in a chair by the window. She reached for the glass of water on the nightstand and noticed her hand was shaking.

"We're having barbecue pork sandwiches for lunch," Caroline said.

"Sounds great."

Caroline wandered to Robin and placed a comforting hand on her shoulder. Robin realized her own mother rarely touched her like this. No, she'd used up all her nurturing energy on Robin's sick, older brother. An ache started low in Robin's stomach.

She went back to Jake's side. "I'll be down in a little while."

Caroline wandered to the door. "He'll be fine, Robin. The doctor said so."

"Thanks." Robin studied Jake's strong face. Stubble was growing from a day without shaving, and his lips were back to their natural color.

As Robin sat in the chair beside the bed, she heard Caroline's sneakers squeak against the wood floor in the hallway.

Jake would be okay, he had to be. It was only hypothermia, not cancer.

Please, God, save my big brother. It was her own voice from when she was a child. The memory filled her chest with grief and regret. Had she not prayed hard enough? Long enough?

Please, God, please.

But God had never answered. After Kyle's death, her family had stopped reaching out to God. They'd shut Him out.

Yet right now, Robin needed that connection more than anything.

Please God, give me strength to help Jake. I care about him in a way I haven't cared for a man in a long time.

Ryan. The memory of her first serious boyfriend flashed to the surface. Ryan was a nice guy with a good career and solid character, but his love of mountain climbing and extreme sports had forced Robin to let him go.

No, that wasn't completely true. It was Robin's fear of losing Ryan to a ten-thousand-foot drop that made her walk away. She'd never told him that. She couldn't admit the truth.

Because she hadn't known it herself. It wasn't until this very moment that she'd realized why she'd pushed Ryan away.

Why she ran from love.

Willing him to wake up, she squeezed Jake's hand. Here was a man who'd saved her life over and over again and put his own life in danger. For her.

Did she have the courage to shelve her fear of loss and open her heart to him? Even if she could, would he want to be anything more than her bodyguard?

Stop going there, she scolded herself. This was a crazy situation, that's all. Still, she wasn't giving up. Not on Jake.

With a long sigh, Jake blinked open his eyes and turned his head toward Robin.

"Hey," he said.

A warm tear trailed down her cheek.

"What's wrong?" he said.

"I was afraid you weren't going to wake up."

"How long have I been out?"

She swiped the tear away.

"About twelve hours."

He glanced down at the blankets, then at her hands clinging to his.

"Sorry, sorry." She released him and placed his hand at his side.

"Don't be sorry." He shot her a smile and motioned for her hand.

She slid her hand into his, and he gently squeezed her fingers. Her chest ached, but it was a good kind of ache. He seemed almost back to normal, or was that wishful thinking on her part?

"Caroline's making lunch," Robin said. "I can bring some up if you'd like."

"No, I'll come down."

"Do you need help with anything?" Suddenly needing space, but not sure why, she slipped her hand from his.

"I'm good. Close the door on your way out."

"Sure, okay. See you downstairs."

She padded across the room.

"Robin?"

She glanced over her shoulder at him.

"Thanks…for holding my hand."

"Sure." With a nod, she shut the door and rushed into her room.

A plethora of emotions clogged her throat from fear to joy to panic. Jake was awake; he really was going to be okay.

She wandered to her bathroom and splashed cold water on her face. She was almost giddy at the thought of a fully-recovered Jake.

"Of course you are. He's keeping you alive."

But that wasn't the cause of her excitement.

She was falling for Jake, falling hard, and feared the pain at the bottom of that fall. First of all, she didn't even know if her feelings were mutual, and secondly, could she risk loving and losing? Would her heart survive?

"First, you'll have to survive Death Eyes," she reminded herself.

The best way to do that was stick with Jake, rely on him, and trust him to help her navigate this terrifying nightmare.

She stared hard at her reflection in the mirror. "I know I can do it, but should I?"

As Jake sat at the kitchen table, he admitted how different everything looked. Robin was more confident, more hopeful than she'd been since he'd known her.

He reminded himself he'd only known her for a few intense days that had brought them closer than the average couple.

Wake up, Jake, you aren't a couple and never will be.

No, he knew how transference worked. It played with your head, caused a victim to think she'd developed deep feelings for a stranger.

Yet, Robin seemed like anything but a victim.

"Need something to drink, water or cola?" she asked him with a smile.

A smile that melted his heart. He snapped his gaze from hers and studied his sandwich. "Water would be great."

He wasn't sure it was wise to keep looking at her, seeing the admiration in her brown eyes when she smiled at him.

Admiration because you're protecting her.

Yet, last night she'd protected him.

He couldn't avoid it any longer. He had to confront her about her actions at the ferry landing.

Little Mack rushed through the kitchen waving a spaceship in his hand, and Caroline gently told him to slow down.

"Got any cookies?" Sketch poured himself a cup of coffee.

"You're too young for coffee," Caroline said. "Try milk with those cookies."

She layered a plate with chocolate chip and oatmeal cookies and set it on the table. Sketch plopped down across from Jake and snatched a cookie as Caroline slid a glass of milk in front of him.

Sketch narrowed his eyes at Jake. "You look like…" He glanced at Caroline who frowned, anticipating Sketch's use of an inappropriate word. "Tired," Sketch said with a grin.

"Excellent sandwich, Caroline," Jake offered, trying to redirect the conversation from his condition. He wanted to take the focus off his failure last night.

The goons had neutralized him, leaving Robin exposed and vulnerable. She could have died.

Because of Jake.

They had gotten the advantage by messing with Jake's head, threatening to interrogate her and kill her. Their cruel words had ripped through Jake's chest and given them the few seconds they'd needed to strike.

Somewhere during the night, Jake had realized his feelings for Robin made him vulnerable. He had to put a stop to his inappropriate feelings for her, but it wouldn't be easy, considering he sensed she was developing feelings for him as well.

She smiled at him as if she read his thoughts. He snapped his attention to Sketch.

"How are the cookies?" Jake asked.

"The chocolate chip rocks." Sketch inhaled two cookies and gulped his milk.

"I want one!" Mack announced, sitting beside Sketch.

"May I have one, please?" Caroline corrected.

"May I have two, please?" Mack said.

They all shared a smile. Jake's heart melted at the perfect scene: family sharing a meal in a nurturing, safe environment.

Something Jake had never experienced growing up.

"Did you get any sleep, honey?" Caroline said, placing a cup of hot tea in front of Robin.

"A few hours," Robin said.

Jake suspected she'd been up all night keeping watch over him. Not good. She could confuse concern for love and then where would they be?

In a huge mess, that's where.

As the family joked and shared their plans for the day, Jake allowed himself to enjoy the fantasy, if only for a few minutes.

Then he shifted in his chair and the stabbing pain of bruised ribs reminded him of their tenuous situation. This is no time for fantasy, not with killers on their trail.

"Chief Wright is going to stop by later," Caroline said.

"I didn't do it," Sketch joked.

"Very funny," Caroline said. "He's coming to see Jake." She turned to Jake. "He wants to know how he can help."

Jake nodded and considered leaving the inn to protect Caroline and the kids. Yet Ethan was the only one who knew they were staying at The Port Whisper Inn, and he wasn't going to betray Jake.

"Well, I have rooms to straighten up," Caroline said. She folded her apron and placed it on the counter. "We'll leave you two alone."

With a knowing smile, Caroline grabbed Mack's hand and motioned at Sketch.

"What?" Sketch said.

"Don't you have work to do outside?" Caroline encouraged.

"Do I?"

Caroline winked and nodded at Jake and Robin. Robin blushed and studied her tea.

"Oh, I get it. They need privacy," Sketch said, making quotation marks with his fingers.

"We have business to discuss," Jake corrected.

"Business, yeah, right." Sketch grabbed a few more cookies and winked. "Have fun with your *business*."

Caroline, Mack and Sketch disappeared, leaving the kitchen oddly quiet. Robin sipped her tea and placed the flowered cup on a saucer. Jake noticed she hadn't finished her sandwich.

"Not hungry?" he said.

"This is a big sandwich. How are you feeling?"

"A little bruised, but okay." He bit into a cookie.

"We were so lucky that the doctor could stop by last night."

Jake nodded and leaned back in his chair, trying not to look directly at Robin. He lost the battle. She looked amazing today with her lightened hair framing her face and her eyes brightened by hope…and something else.

"Robin, we should talk," he started.

"No lectures."

He studied her. "What do you mean?"

"I know where this is going, Jake. I did what I had to last night to help you and I won't apologize for it."

That shut him down. But just for a second. "Robin, it was unwise to—"

"I disagree. You've saved my life multiple times and I had the chance to do the same for you. I wasn't going to abandon you."

"Your job is to take care of yourself, first and foremost."

"I was taking care of myself. I've got a better chance of surviving all this with you beside me."

With you beside me. The words tore at his chest as he found himself wishing she meant something other than Jake acting as bodyguard.

"You had the car keys. You could have left without putting yourself at risk," he said.

"I wouldn't have left you. Sorry. New topic."

"Aren't you bossy?"

She shrugged and bit back a yawn.

"You didn't sleep at all last night, did you?" he asked.

"I slept." She glanced back at her tea. "I also remembered. Everything."

"Everything as in…?"

"My life, my childhood. My brother died of cancer when I was eleven."

"I'm sorry." He wanted to reach out and hold her hand, tell her how sorry he was that she had to relive the grief of losing her brother all over again.

"Thanks. It explains a lot."

"Like?"

"Why I keep people at a distance. Why I didn't believe in God."

"And now you do?"

She shrugged. "It gave me comfort to pray last night when I was worried about you."

"I'm glad," he said, glad that she'd found solace in prayer.

"We gave up on God years ago after Kyle died. It just seemed pointless."

"Faith is never pointless."

"Yeah." She glanced up at him. "I'm learning that by hanging out with you."

Hanging out. He wished they were simply hanging out and not hiding from danger. Maybe this was a good opportunity to remind her of their purpose for being together.

"Robin, we're not just hanging out. Remember why we're here."

"Meaning what?"

"I don't want you to confuse our relationship with something more than it is."

Her expression hardened, and she stood, taking her teacup to the sink. He'd hurt her, and wanted to take the words back, but they both had to stay focused on reality if they wanted to survive.

"You're saying if we'd met in another situation, at church or through friends, you wouldn't be interested in—" she paused "—dating me?"

He wasn't sure what to say. He wouldn't lie, and, the truth was, he would be honored to date a woman like Robin.

"We didn't meet through friends," he said. "We need to stay grounded in reality, Robin."

"Reality, right." She stood at the sink, gazing out the window into the backyard.

Tense silence stretched between them. He hated the silence, hated that he'd caused her pain.

Jake stood and went to her. "Robin, I'm sorry."

She turned, wrapped her arms around his waist and placed her head against his chest. Instead of hurting his bruised ribs, her embrace seemed to heal him from the inside, and he found himself hugging her in return.

Talk about a mixed message. One minute he was pushing her away, and the next he was hugging her, stroking her back. But he couldn't let go.

The shrill sound of a ringing phone echoed through the kitchen. Neither of them moved. They held onto each other, wishing for something that could never be.

After a few rings, the kitchen grew silent again. Jake closed his eyes and found himself praying for the ability to get his perspective back and for strength to put distance between them without hurting her.

Footsteps pounded down the main stairs and the kitchen door swung open. Jake broke the embrace and glanced at Caroline, who stood in the doorway.

She hesitated, realizing she'd interrupted a tender moment. "It's Ethan. He needs to speak with you."

Jake brushed his hand against Robin's arm. "You okay?" he asked.

She nodded, turning back to the window.

Jake took the phone and stepped onto the back porch. "Hey, Ethan."

"You guys okay?"

Jake glanced through the window and spotted Caroline rubbing Robin's back.

"We've been better. Your sketch artist never showed."

"I know. He's missing."

"How did they know he was coming to meet us?"

"I've worked with him before. They must have figured that out and had him under surveillance."

"They almost got Robin."

"But you stopped them."

"No, she did. And there's more. She remembers everything. I'm thinking maybe even small details from the shooting. I haven't asked yet. I was pretty out of it until an hour ago. They got the jump on me."

"On you?" Ethan said, shocked.

"Long story. What's next?"

"I'm working off the grid on this one. I spoke with Edwards's wife. We found a lock box in the basement, but no key. I have to figure out a way to break in. I think he was onto some kind of department corruption, Jake."

"Where does that leave Robin?"

"In limbo, until I can build a case. Any details you can get from her about that night could help."

"I'll talk to her."

"Also, Robin's friend, Jenn, the one who visited her at the hospital?"

"Yeah?"

"She was mugged this morning."

"Is she okay?"

"A little bruised, but yeah. There's more."

Jake waited, gripping the phone.

"Someone's trying to make it look like Robin gave the killer access to the building. It was a key card from the pediatric foundation that opened the door to the Remmington office."

"That's not possible, E."

"I don't believe she's involved, but a week ago, I thought I could trust my guys. Makes me think anything's possible, Jake."

Anything's possible, even love in the most stressful of situations?

Jake shook his head to get his bearings back.

"They're turning up the heat, like they think Robin knows something or saw something that could bring everything crashing down," Ethan said.

"What do you want us to do?" Jake asked.

"Stay alive."

TWELVE

Robin knew the instant Jake walked into the room that the situation had grown more serious. She'd learned to read his moods and his expressions, and this one made her tense.

"What is it?" she asked.

"Ethan had an update. We should talk."

"Why don't the two of you take a drive out to the state park for some privacy and watch the sailboats. I always find that relaxing, and there are plenty of isolated spots for talking."

"Are you up to it?" she asked Jake. Truth was, whatever bad news he was about to drop on her, she'd rather hear it while they were alone, away from Caroline and the kids.

"That's probably a good idea," Jake said. "Let's get our jackets."

"Oh, are we dressing as the respectable couple again?" Robin kidded, nerves tangling her stomach in knots.

"No, you're fine the way you are," he said, eyeing her jeans and T-shirt.

Caroline gave Robin an extra fleece jacket, and handed Jake the keys. "Wait a second, I'll pack you some snacks."

As Caroline scurried around the kitchen, Robin searched Jake's eyes for some hint of how bad the situation had become. He studied the keys to the Impala in his hand, and, when he finally glanced up, he shot her a forced smile.

Oh boy. This was not good.

"There, some cookies, fruit and cheese." Caroline handed Robin the insulated bag.

"Thanks." Robin gave her a hug, suddenly worried that she may not see the woman again, that Jake might tell Robin they had to go on the run.

She and Jake went out back to the car. "You want me to drive?" she said.

"Nope, I'm good."

They got in the car and headed for the park.

"Do you want to talk about it?" she said.

"When we get there."

Robin leaned against the seat and glanced out the window trying to focus on the beauty of the trees bordering the road. The sun peeked through, and she shut her eyes against its brightness.

Jake turned on the radio to a soft country station and she found herself drifting immediately into another world. The vocalist sang about true love and painful memories. Robin's imagination filled her mind with images of Jake holding her in his arms, guiding her around a dance floor.

I don't want you to confuse our relationship with something more than it is.

She repeated Jake's words in her head, but they couldn't compete with the romantic song playing on the radio.

She realized he didn't give her a direct answer when she'd asked if they'd met in different circumstances, would they have dated. Did that mean he shared the feelings growing between them?

With my arm around my love... I have everything I need...

The lyrics inspired her daydream. Jake took her hand and led her outside onto a long, wooden porch. They held hands, looking into each other's eyes. His eyes sparkled as he smiled and squeezed her hands.

"Robin, I—"

A bang echoed from behind Jake, and his eyes popped wide,

a red stain growing across his pressed, white shirt. Jake coughed and fell to his knees.

"Jake!"

Grinning, pointing his gun at Robin, Death Eyes stood at the other end of the porch.

"No!"

"Robin? Wake up."

She gasped and opened her eyes, panicked. She must have fallen asleep.

"Hey, it's okay, sweetheart," Jake said. "We're at the park."

She glanced out the window at the mass of water stretching to the horizon. It took her a second to figure out she was awake, this was real and the shooting was only a nightmare.

"Robin?" Jake tipped her face and looked at her with gorgeous blue-green eyes, the same eyes that had been startled and wide, clouded with death, in her nightmare.

"I'm fine." She snapped her attention from him and flung open the door. Had to get out, away from Jake and the pain of seeing him hurt. Killed.

"You want to talk about it?" he said, walking up beside her.

"Not now." She hugged herself.

"Okay, then let's find a spot to talk."

She nodded, and they started down a dirt trail leading closer to the water. Water always calmed her, another memory that had returned during the night. She would sit on the shore at Magnuson Park and watch the sailboats drift across Lake Washington for hours. She'd bring books and lose herself in the beautiful weather and peaceful sound of waves lapping against the shore. Sometimes she'd bring a knitting project or business journals, or she'd write letters to college friends and make up checklists for work.

But she'd never just sit and think. It was too dangerous. She might end up in that place, that dark place.

I didn't pray hard enough. I'm not as smart as Kyle, as good as Kyle. As lovable.

She took a quick breath and shook her head.

"You okay?" Jake said.

"Sure, okay." But she couldn't look at him. Not yet.

The pain welled in her chest. Not pain at the thought of being shot herself, but at the thought of losing Jake.

She pumped her fists, trying to change her mood and jar herself out of the dark whirlwind she was getting sucked into.

"How about over there?" Jake pointed to a spot surrounded by trees, overlooking the water.

"Looks great."

They had started in the direction of the bluff, when Robin heard voices echo down the trail. Jake pulled her behind a cedar tree. He was being extra cautious, since no one could possibly know they were here.

He's extra cautious. He's a warrior, a fighter. He's not going to be fatally injured.

Yet last night he was bested by the two men after Robin. He could have...died.

A couple passed without noticing Jake and Robin. Once they were out of sight, Jake took her hand and led her back onto the path.

"This is perfect," he said softly.

Again, whimsy burst into her mind: Jake taking her for a romantic stroll along a rocky shore, holding hands, laughing, enjoying each other's company. Her lack of sleep was catching up with her.

They stepped around a few trees and found a small clearing where others must come for peace and quiet.

What Robin felt churning in her stomach was anything but peace.

She slipped her hand from his. "It's beautiful out here."

A few large rocks made for perfect chairs. Robin sat on one and interlaced her fingers. "So, before you drop the bomb about Ethan's phone call, can I ask you something?"

Jake sat on a rock a few feet away. "Sure."

"What happened last night?"

He studied her. "What do you mean?"

She should stop now, but couldn't help herself. She had to know.

"Those men, how did they get the jump on you?" she asked.

He broke eye contact and glanced across the water.

"Jake?"

"I'm sorry. Truly."

"Don't be sorry. Just, tell me what happened. Did they surprise you or threaten you or—"

"They threatened you, okay?" He pinned her with intense eyes.

"I've been threatened ever since the shooting. Why was this—"

"They were very clear about their plans to kill you, and I lost my focus." He stood and paced a few feet away. "That's what happens when you get personally involved."

Involved, as in… He *did* care about her.

As if he read her thoughts, he turned to her. "Which is why we can't get involved. I've said it four or five times, but you're not getting it. So here's the deal. Things are worse for you right now. Ethan said someone's making it look like you gave the killer access to the office where the cop was killed."

"What?" Robin jumped to her feet.

"And your friend, Jenn? She was mugged this morning."

"Jenn?" Her voice grew hushed. "Why would they—"

"Because they're trying to get to you any way they can. They make you a suspect in order to arrest you, hurt your friend so you'll come out of hiding, threaten to interrogate and kill you to weaken my ability to protect you."

"Jenn," she whispered. "It's not fair. It's my fault."

"No, it isn't."

"I have to call her."

"Not right now. You have to listen to me and stay focused on fighting back."

Confusion warred with frustration. "I wouldn't have let anyone into the office, and there's no reason for them to hurt Jenn. She's my friend and—"

I don't have a lot of friends.

She couldn't admit it, not to Jake. Not to anyone, even herself. Until now.

Of course not, if she let someone get too close, it would hurt that much more when they were gone.

"I know I failed you last night, but that won't happen again." Jake placed his hands on her shoulders.

"Why, because you're not going to let yourself get personally involved?"

"Yeah, pretty much."

"Good luck with that." Because she knew she was already involved and then some. Her chest ached with the love growing in her heart, tainted by the realization she'd lose Jake, too.

"Robin, it's the only way to protect you."

And the only way to protect myself.

No, she was tired of running from close relationships because she'd lost her brother. How long was she going to let her past control her life?

"Back to Ethan's phone call," she said, wanting to change the direction of the conversation.

"Anything you can remember from that night, any details, could help Ethan put the pieces together."

"If the cops think I let the killer in, aren't they looking for me?"

"Probably, but nothing official, yet." Jake sat on the rock, she noticed, a few inches closer than before. "Are you up to remembering details about that night?"

"I guess." She shelved her anxiety. Jake was here; he'd hold her hand and protect her.

"Okay, so start with when you were at work," Jake said.

"I got there about eight. I needed hard-copy lists for the walk-athon and my printer had died at home, so I went into the office." Her gaze drifted to the sailboats, so peaceful, drifting across water, powered by the wind. "I was going to print out the lists and leave, but I got caught up in work. More participants signed up for the walk, so I decided to process them instead of waiting until the next morning. I lost track of time, and, a few hours later, about nine, I packed up."

"You didn't notice anything strange or hear anything?"

"No, not really."

"Continue."

"Jenn called, scolding me for being at work. She said I *so* shouldn't be there on a Friday night. Anyway a group of work friends were waiting for me," she paused and looked at Jake. "I told her I was leaving and started for the elevators and… That's when I saw it."

"What did you see, exactly?"

"That man, from last night, the one I call Death Eyes."

"The bald one?" he said.

"Yes."

"Okay. Close your eyes. It might help you remember."

She gripped the hem of her fleece.

"Robin?" Jake took her hand and squeezed. "You're safe. You can do this."

She closed her eyes. Grounded by the warmth of his hands, she whipped up as much courage as she could and replayed that night in her head.

Light streamed through an office down the hall.

She glanced right.

Officer Edwards raised his hands.

Bang!

She dropped her phone and froze, her gaze shot up to Death Eyes.

The gun.

And another man dodging out of sight.

She opened her eyes. "Jake, someone else was there."

"Who?"

"I don't know, but I recognize him from someplace." Robin stood and paced to the overlook. "I don't know from where, but I can see his face."

"You think he's a public figure or someone you worked with?"

"Public figure, I think."

"It's okay." He came up behind her. "It's a good lead. We should try and figure out who he is, maybe look through news stories. Come on, let's head back."

She glanced longingly at the Strait of Juan De Fuca, wishing they could stay and actually enjoy the beautiful weather.

"Robin?"

"For a few minutes, before I remembered, I felt like everything was normal again. You know." She glanced up at him. "Safe."

"It will be. I promise."

He pulled her against his chest, and she resisted the urge to lecture him on mixed messages. One minute he was all business, the next, he was hugging her.

As if he read her mind, he broke the embrace, but didn't let go of her hand. "Let's go."

He led her down the trail back to the car. Relief and sadness washed over her. She was relieved that the memory was growing clearer, which would help her identify the criminals and put an end to this nightmare. On the other hand, once it was over, she and Jake would be over. They'd have no reason to be together, holding hands, hugging each other.

Maybe it was for the best. If she didn't love, she couldn't be hurt.

God, am I crazy?

Here she was, asking for God's guidance again. But it felt natural and calmed her nerves.

They turned a corner overlooking the parking lot, and Jake stopped short. "Hang on."

She followed the direction of his gaze. Two men were circling Caroline's car.

THIRTEEN

Jake crouched behind a cedar tree and shifted Robin behind him.

"Do you think…?" Robin said, not finishing her sentence.

But Jake knew the question: Were they connected to the thugs who'd attacked Jake last night?

"Not necessarily," Jake said, eyeing the men. They weren't the same men from last night, but that didn't mean they weren't a part of this.

"How did they find us?" she said.

"We don't know they're connected to the shooting."

"What if they stopped by the inn and…and…"

He stroked her arm. "Shh. Don't go there. They could be looking at the car for any number of reasons," he said, trying to convince himself.

He watched the men give Caroline's Chevy Impala the once-over, peering in the windows and eyeing the body. A sheriff's patrol car cruised through the lot and stopped behind the Impala.

"Robin, take this." He pulled out Morgan's card and put it in her hand.

"Why?" She looked at him with frightened eyes.

"A cop is down there. It's my chance to figure out what's going on."

"You're not leaving me behind."

"Just for a minute. Please, honey, trust me on this. I'm ninety-nine percent sure this isn't related to the case, but I need to be positive and keep you safe."

"Jake—"

"Do you trust me to protect you?"

"Yes."

"Then stay here while I check it out. If anything strange happens, find a pay phone and call Morgan, got it?"

She nodded.

He kissed her on the forehead and turned quickly to leave. If he stared one more second into those amazing eyes, he'd completely lose his focus.

Walking down the trail, he took note of everything about the men, from height and weight to facial features and clothing. They were in their mid-twenties, dressed for hiking. As he got closer, he noticed the deputy analyzing their drivers' licenses.

"Can I help you?" Jake said.

"This your car?" the deputy asked, passing the licenses back to the men.

"A friend's," Jake said. "She let me take it for a ride on this beautiful day. Why, is there a problem?"

"How about some ID?"

"Sure." Jake pulled out his driver's license. As the cop looked it over, Jake noticed that the two guys seemed nervous. "Is there a problem, deputy?" he repeated.

He handed Jake his license and glanced at the men. "We've had some burglaries at the park, and I spotted these two hanging around your car."

"It's awesome," the one guy offered. "Think your friend's interested in selling?"

"Shut up, Ray." His friend elbowed him in the ribs.

"It has sentimental value, so I doubt it," Jake said. "It was her late husband's pride and joy."

"Bummer," Ray said.

"Break-ins, huh?" Ray's friend asked the deputy.

"Three last week."

"We're here to hike, officer," Ray's friend said.

The sound of a call echoed from his radio in the deputy's car. "Have a good day." He got into the cruiser and pulled out.

The two hikers weren't so anxious to leave.

"Where'd he find this thing?" Ray said, running his hands across the hood. "It's mint."

Jake needed to get Robin back to the inn where they could start investigating the stranger she remembered from the shooting.

"Why don't you give me your number in case my friend changes her mind about selling?" Jake offered.

"Really?" Ray said.

"Sure, anything's possible for the right price," Jake said, trying to get them to move on, so he could get Robin home safely.

Ray pulled out a convenience store receipt and jotted down a number. "Cool. Thanks."

"Yep." Jake slipped it into his shirt pocket, then patted his other pocket and his jeans pockets. "Huh. I must have dropped my cell up on the ridge."

"Come on. Let's go, Ray."

"Okay. Hey, thanks again," Ray called.

Jake waved and headed back to Robin's hiding spot. He didn't turn around until he was out of view.

He glanced back and spotted the men wandering toward a trailhead. Jake glanced back and spotted Robin crouching, her hands clenched in prayer, her eyes closed.

"Robin?" he said.

"You're okay." She launched herself into his arms and clung tight.

Every time she did that, his body warmed with an indescribable sense of peace. Not possible and definitely not good. For either of them.

"They were just admiring the Impala."

She broke the embrace and glanced at the parking lot. Ray and his buddy and disappeared up the trail.

"And the cop?" she said.

"There've been some break-ins and he was checking them out, thought they might be the perps. Come on."

He took her hand, a new and automatic response to being with her.

"I kept praying and praying..." Her voice trailed off.

"And it helped," Jake finished for her.

She got in the car, and he closed the door, then scanned the area. He couldn't be too careful. A smart predator would send guys like Ray and his buddy to investigate, seemingly innocent men that wouldn't raise any flags in Jake's mind.

Then again, everyone was a red flag.

Even Robin. But for a completely different reason.

Jake kept checking the rearview mirror as they drove back, but no one followed them. He calmed Robin down by suggesting that her remembering the second man at the scene was a big break in the case.

"That was quick," Caroline said as they entered the kitchen.

"Has anyone been asking about us, or have any new guests checked in?" Jake asked.

"I thought you said we were safe," Robin said.

"We can't be too cautious." He glanced at Caroline.

"No new guests, and no one's asked about you." She eyed Jake. "Did something happen?"

"Two men were checking out your car, but I don't think they're a threat," Jake said.

"Checking it out?"

"They were admiring it."

"Yes, well, Thomas took good care of his baby." She smiled. "But why didn't you stay out longer? It's such a beautiful day."

"I remembered something about the shooting," Robin said.

"Is Sketch downstairs?" Jake asked.

"Yes."

"Good, I think he can help."

Jake opened the door and started downstairs. "Sketch?" Jake called, but the kid didn't answer. He was wearing headphones and tapping a pen against the desk. They went downstairs, and Jake touched his shoulder. The kid practically jumped out of his chair.

"Dude, don't ever do that to a person," Sketch said, breathing heavy.

"Sorry, you couldn't hear me with the headphones on."

"Yeah, yeah, okay. What's up?"

"Robin remembered seeing someone at the scene of the shooting, and we need to figure out who it was."

"Ah, you came to the right computer geek. I've got facial design software." Sketch plopped back down in his swivel chair.

"How did you get that?" Jake said.

"You'd be surprised what you can find on the internet." He motioned for Robin to pull up a chair. "At your service, pretty lady." He glanced at Jake. "Sorry."

"What, for stating the obvious?"

Robin blushed and glanced at her hands in her lap.

"Let's get started," Jake said. "I'd like to send something to Ethan today, if possible."

"May I call Jenn first to make sure she's okay?" Robin said with hope in her eyes.

"Sure," Jake said.

Sketch slipped the phone from his top drawer, popped a battery in the back and handed it to Robin. "Keep it to ninety seconds just to be extra careful."

"How does it work?" Jake asked Sketch as Robin called her friend.

"It bounces all over the place like that game, Spirograph. Boing, boing, boing. You never know where the call comes from."

"And you created this because...?"

"I was bored?" Sketch shrugged. "It's not hurting anyone."

No, and, actually, it had been a lifesaver for Jake and Robin. He could call Ethan without putting them in danger, and Robin could ease her mind by checking in with her friend.

"Hey, Jenn?…I know, I'm so sorry. I'm okay, promise…"

Jake wanted to give her privacy to speak with her friend, but was still on edge and couldn't help himself. He had hated leaving her hiding behind the cedar tree in the park, but he had been unable to risk the possibility that the strangers were more than car enthusiasts.

"No, I'm safe. I'm with Jake.… Who said that? Did you get his badge number…? That's wrong. I trust him." She glanced up at Jake. "I'm sure. It's almost like I'm on vacation.… Yes."

Jake motioned for her to wind it up; he wasn't sure why. Instinct, perhaps?

"Okay, I've gotta go. Promise… You. too."

She handed the phone back to Sketch. He pressed a few buttons, popped out the battery and put it in his drawer.

Robin shot Jake a worried glance. "She said the police officer who interviewed her thinks you kidnapped me."

"Doesn't surprise me," Jake said. "Ethan's the only one who knows what's really going on."

"What if they put a bulletin out on you, and you get arrested?"

Jake placed his hand on her shoulder. "No one's going to find us here."

He hoped. How could they? No, he couldn't go there. He had to focus on taking the offensive and using her recovered memories to identify all the players in this conspiracy.

"Whenever you guys are ready," Sketch prompted.

"Okay, wait a second." Robin closed her eyes and pressed her fingertips to her temples. "He looks like…Cary Grant. Kind of."

"Who?" Sketch said.

"Google him," Jake suggested.

"Kind of a long, angular face, dark hair, dark eyes. He was wearing a suit. It looked expensive."

The teenager created a four-quadrant image of the outline of a man's head. He opened another window in his browser and searched Cary Grant. Images popped up.

"Sunken-in eyes or high forehead or anything like that?" Sketch asked.

"Deep-set eyes, thin lips." She opened her eyes and looked at Sketch. "And a slight beard."

"Awesome. This will be easier than we thought."

They worked on the image for a solid hour, Sketch asking her questions and Robin calmly answering him.

"Anyone thirsty?" Caroline called from the top of the stairs.

"I could use some water," Robin said.

"I'll have a beer," Sketch said. "Kidding! You got any lemonade?"

"Sure. I'll bring it down."

"No, I'll get it." Jake left Robin and Sketch to work on the image and went upstairs.

"How's it going down there?" Caroline said, pouring Sketch's glass of lemonade.

"Pretty good. I'm hoping if she remembers the guy, Ethan can use that to solve this case."

She placed the glasses on a tray and turned to Jake. "And then?"

"And then she gets her life back." He rolled his neck.

"What happens to your life?"

"Everything gets back to normal. For everyone."

Caroline leaned against the counter and crossed her arms over her chest. "She saved your life last night. She cares about you, Jake."

"She's grateful."

"Why can't you accept the fact you might have found something special here?"

"Because I'm a realist."

"You're running scared, but of what? She's a sweet girl. You're not going to break her."

"You sure about that?"

"You're not him, Jake. You're nothing like your father."

He wished he could believe her. He wanted to deny that part of himself, deny the possibility of getting close and hurting the woman he loved. It could happen. Genes were genes. And he had his father's.

"Your father had a drinking problem," she said. "You don't drink. Your father had a rage problem. I've never seen you angry a day in your life."

"You didn't live with me, and you didn't see me in the service."

"You did what your job required you to do."

"I'll take these downstairs." He reached for the tray, but she blocked him.

"Honey, please stop punishing yourself for your father's sins."

"I don't know what you mean."

"You blame yourself for not being able to protect your mom. I saw it in your eyes whenever you looked at her."

He snapped his gaze to meet Caroline's. "Can you explain something to me?"

She nodded.

"Why didn't she leave? I mean, she had plenty of opportunities. She had relatives in Oregon. We could have—"

"She loved you too much."

"That makes no sense."

"Your father knew something about your mom and threatened to use it to get custody."

"What could he possibly know that would give him custody?"

"She had a slight breakdown years before you were born, when your grandmother died. Your mom was seventeen and her father, your grandfather, didn't know how to console her, so he had her committed."

"Because of her grief?"

"Yes. When she got out a few weeks later, she found comfort and healed through prayer and by getting involved in church. She married your dad, not knowing he had a violent temper. He found out she was planning to leave him and threatened to take you away. She loved you and Amy so much."

"Maybe too much."

"Don't say that."

"She shouldn't have sacrificed herself for us like that."

"You'd do the same thing for someone you loved."

"I'm sorry, I..." Robin said from the doorway.

Jake glanced at her.

"We're finished if you want to take a look. Sorry, I didn't mean to..." She pointed over her shoulder. "I'll be downstairs."

She disappeared into the basement. He wondered how much of the conversation she'd heard. This was the most he'd talked to anyone about his dad since Mom's death.

"I'll take this down." Jake grabbed the tray.

Caroline touched his shirtsleeve. "Love is complicated, Jake, but don't deny your feelings because of your father. If you do, then he wins."

With a nod, he made for the stairs. "Caroline?"

"Yes?"

"Thanks."

"My pleasure."

Jake carried the tray down to Sketch and Robin and slid it onto an upturned crate. "Refreshments," he said, not making eye contact with Robin. He felt raw and off balance.

His father had threatened to take Jake and Amy away? Why? It wasn't as if the old man liked his kids, or paid any attention to them, for that matter.

No, it had been a power thing. Power over his wife, Jake's loving and fragile mom.

She'd always hide Jake and Amy when Dad had his rages. And when Jake was a teenager, she made him promise never to physically engage his father, even though Jake knew he could take him down. She feared what his dad might do, like file charges against his own son.

Promise me, she'd say with tears in her eyes. He couldn't disobey her. He'd loved her so.

Yet, even in the end, as her body lost its battle with cancer, she and Jake had never talked about it. She'd only told him he was a good boy, a loving son and would make a wonderful husband someday.

If he'd been a loving son, he would have protected her from Dad. Why hadn't she let him?

She loved you too much.

"Jake?" Robin touched his arm, bringing him back, grounding him.

"Yeah, sorry."

"You want to look at this or what?" Sketch said.

Jake stepped up to the computer and studied the screen.

The phone rang, and Sketch glanced at the caller ID. "I think it's your friend, Ethan."

Sketch handed Jake the phone. "Ethan, good timing," Jake said. "Robin remembered someone else at the scene, and we've created a pretty good likeness. Where should I send it?"

"Don't, in case they trace your IP address."

"We've got that covered," Jake said. "Where do you want me to send it?"

"My cell phone. I'll get it faster." Ethan rattled off the number and Jake relayed it to Sketch.

"Listen, I got into Edwards's lock box," Ethan said. "He had a ton of cash, plus manifests for shipments of the synthetic drug that's being smuggled into Seattle, probably through Remmington Imports."

"So, he *was* dirty?"

"I'm not convinced. I think he was undercover, way under, and was collecting evidence to build a case."

"Says the eternal optimist."

"Yeah, well, I can't talk my way out of this guilt trip; the sketch artist was found a few hours ago passed out in his car. They're checking him out at the hospital, but I'll bet he was drugged, probably with the same drug they're smuggling."

"You any closer to knowing who's behind this?"

"Not sure. I'm calling my attorney brother, Alex, to cover my back."

"Shouldn't you take this up the chain of command?"

"I'm still not sure who I can trust in the department."

Jake glanced at Robin, feeling bad that this lovely woman had fallen into a pile of trouble just for being in the wrong place at the wrong time.

"Hang on, I'm getting your email," Ethan said.

A few seconds passed.

"Jake? Is Robin sure about this?"

"Yeah, why?"

"I've seen this guy."

"Who is he?"

"Wait. I'm getting a text."

"What's going on?" Robin asked.

"Not sure. Looks like this is related to drug smuggling." He pointed to the computer screen. "Find everything you can on Remmington Imports," he ordered Sketch.

The kid saluted.

"Jake, I'm back. I've got bad news. They've issued a BOLO for Robin Strand."

FOURTEEN

Which meant every law enforcement agency in the State of Washington would be on the lookout for Robin.

"As a suspect?" Jake asked Ethan.

"More like a missing person, but I'm not going to lie. She is a person of interest, Jake."

"I'm not bringing her in."

"I understand how you feel, but I'm an officer of the law and need to follow protocol."

Jake gripped the phone. "Meaning what?"

"I'm officially ordering you to bring her back."

"And unofficially?"

"Just…" Ethan paused. "I'll call you later, after I look into a few things."

"Thanks." He handed Sketch the phone.

"What happened?" Robin said. "Did he recognize the sketch?"

"I think so, but we got distracted. They've issued a BOLO for you."

"BOLO?"

"Be on the lookout," Sketch explained. "It's like an All Points Bulletin, sent to law enforcement agencies, so they can find you and arrest you."

"I'm not the bad guy." Robin folded her arms over her chest.

Jake admired her strong reaction as opposed to falling apart.

"It doesn't matter," Jake said. "Two police officers are dead, and you're their best lead."

"Tough. I'm not going back. I'm not going to let them lock me up where Death Eyes can get to me. I'll run. I'll run and hide and—"

"Stop, okay?" Jake said, placing his hand on her shoulder. "We're not going back."

"But Detective Beck knows where we are."

"He's not going to tell anyone. He's got his hands full trying to figure out who in the department is involved in this."

"Speaking of *this*, I've got background on the key players at Remmington Imports," Sketch said.

"Good. Print it out, and I'll look it over."

Robin held his gaze, still upset. He couldn't blame her. This case was spinning out of control, and even Ethan was unable to get a handle on it.

"I just don't want to feel terrified all the time," Robin muttered.

"Why don't you go upstairs and help Caroline? It will take your mind off things."

With a frustrated nod, Robin went upstairs and shut the door.

"You gonna get her out of this in one piece?" Sketch asked.

"That's the plan."

And he'd better, and not just because he'd made a promise to protect her. He caught himself slipping, and this time didn't fight it. Caroline's words had opened his heart to the possibility of love, and now nothing was going to block that secret wish.

"Earth to Macho Man. Hello, Macho Man?" Sketch said with a raised eyebrow.

"I need to call Morgan."

"Who?"

"Chief Wright."

The kid shuddered. "Cops hate me on principle."

"Why? You're not doing anything illegal, are you?"

Sketch put up his hands. "No, honest. But I'm a dropout, and they know it. It's like they can smell it on me."

More like Sketch was disappointed in himself for not finishing high school.

"Can you call the police, non-emergency?" Jake asked.

"Don't bring him down here," Sketch said, panicked.

"I won't. Promise."

Jake called Morgan and asked him to swing by. When he went upstairs, he found Robin helping Caroline bake scones for the next morning's breakfast.

"Where are you going?" Robin asked, rolling the dough.

"Outside for a second. Morgan's stopping by."

"The police chief?"

"Yep. I need to fill him in."

Robin froze. "What if he wants to arrest me?"

Caroline chuckled. "Now, why would Morgan do that? For making extra-fattening scones?"

Jake and Robin shared a glance. "He won't arrest you, Robin," Jake assured. "But I need him to know what's going on."

He went out front and leaned against the porch railing. It didn't take long for Morgan to pull up in his cruiser.

"Hey, you look pretty good, considering," Morgan said. "You looked like you'd been hit by a Mack truck last night."

"Thanks for helping with that."

"I was hoping you'd call." Morgan sat on a porch chair and slipped off his sunglasses.

"It's time I filled you in about what's happening on the other side of the water."

"With Ethan's case?"

"Yep. He just called. It's pretty bad. Possible police corruption involving a synthetic-drug smuggling operation."

"How's the girl involved? A very pretty girl, I might add. Man, was she worried about you last night."

"Of course she was worried. I'm the guy that's going to keep her from being killed."

"If you say so." He winked. "So, back to business. What can I do to help?"

"Keep an eye out for the thugs who found us last night. One's tall and bald with dark eyes, the other stocky with bad skin."

"No problem."

"They've issued a BOLO on Robin, but Ethan doesn't know who to trust. I'm afraid it might be a ploy to get her back, so they can kill her." Jake hesitated. "If you get one describing a female, late twenties, dark brown hair and brown eyes…"

"Can't ignore a BOLO, so I'll be on the lookout for a brunette." He winked. "If I see the guys who jumped you, should I arrest them?"

"No, don't. Morgan, they're—"

"What, out of my league?" he smiled.

"I didn't say that."

"I'll turn on my small-town cop charm and tell them about the couple that headed west to the coast. That work?"

"Hopefully, you won't have to charm anybody."

"Ah, but I need practice. I haven't had a date in three months."

"Better than me."

"I don't know." Morgan glanced through the front window. "I'll bet she'd date you, if you asked."

"This is business."

"Yeah, well." Morgan stood. "Once your business is over, you'd better ask her out, or I'm going to." He flashed his million-dollar grin. "You got a cell phone?"

"Ditched it in the city."

"Have Caroline pick you up a throwaway in case you need to call me."

They shook hands, and Morgan didn't immediately let go. "I'm glad you're okay, man. Let's keep it that way."

"Thanks."

With a two-finger salute, Morgan sauntered off the front porch and got in his patrol car.

As he drove off, Jake's gaze wandered to the playground across the street. He could almost see himself, Morgan and Ethan playing army guys on the jungle gym, firing off rounds at the enemy, barking orders, pretending to save the world from an alien enemy.

They were a team, and Jake realized the relationship he had with Morgan and E were his closest and most intimate.

Until he'd met Robin.

No, a seventy-two hour entanglement was not the same as a relationship.

"How'd it go?" Robin's sweet voice said, as she stepped onto the porch.

"Good. He knows enough to help keep us safe without compromising himself."

"You're always worried about the other guy, aren't you?"

"Morgan was a good friend when we were kids," he said, focused on the playground. "Mom would bring us here for vacation and for that one week a year…"

"What?"

She touched his cheek, and, closing his eyes, he leaned into her touch. He couldn't help himself. "For that one week all the bad stuff went away. That's why this place is so…"

"Magical?"

He blinked his eyes open and looked at her. He lost himself in her compassionate expression. "Yeah, magical."

"I know what you mean." She leaned forward and kissed him.

Robin wasn't sure what had gotten into her, but she couldn't help herself. She needed to let Jake know that, no matter what happened, if they lived or died, she cared about him. A lot.

She was prepared for him to push her away, but instead he

gripped her shoulders ever-so-gently, and she could feel his inaudible sigh.

Then he broke the kiss, pulled her against his chest and whispered in her ear. "We shouldn't have done that."

"Maybe not, but I needed to." She broke the embrace and looked up into his eyes. "This isn't some kind of psychological condition, Jake. I care about you, and not just because you're my bodyguard. I needed you to know that."

With a nod, he pulled her close again.

He couldn't say the words back, but she was okay with that. She felt in his touch how much he cared about her. This wasn't just business for him, either. It was more, and it could be much more, if they got through this safely.

The front door swung open with a crash. "I got some—whoa, sorry," Sketch said, backing up.

"It's okay." Jake released Robin and eyed Sketch. "What have you got?"

"I can come back later if you lovebirds need to finish your… whatever it is." He motioned with his hand.

Jake smiled at Robin, and her heart melted. He had such a wonderful smile, something she suspected he didn't share with many people.

"Back to work," he said to her. "Why don't you finish helping Caroline?"

"Sure." They went back into the house, and Jake disappeared with Sketch downstairs.

Robin leaned against the kitchen counter, still feeling his warmth on her lips. She'd never been kissed like that, or held like that—such a gentle touch from a tough guy.

"Don't listen to him," Caroline blurted out.

"Excuse me?"

"If he pushes you away, you push back." Caroline put the last of the scones in the oven and turned to Robin. "He's a complicated man, but he cares deeply about you. I can tell."

"He says I feel this way because of the case, my life being in danger and all that."

"He'll say just about anything to keep anyone from getting too close. It's a defense mechanism."

Yeah, Robin knew the tactic only too well. Hadn't she done the same thing with Ryan? Let him get close and, once he did, she pushed him away to distance herself from emotional intimacy and potential pain.

"What is it?" Caroline said, studying Robin.

Robin shook her head. "We're more alike than he knows."

"Maybe that's a good thing. You can understand him, have patience where someone else might not."

Caroline cleared off the kitchen table and started folding clean linens from a basket on the floor.

Robin joined her, hoping for more insight into Jake. "Did he ever have a serious girlfriend?"

"Yes, although I question how serious it was in her mind."

"What do you mean?" Robin pulled a crisp, white sheet from the basket.

"Jake's mom and I had our theories on Cassandra."

"How long did they date?"

Caroline frowned. "Too long."

"Bad, huh?"

Caroline hesitated as she placed a folded sheet on the kitchen table. "That girl liked to play head games, and Jake, well, what you see is what you get. He's a good man with a cautious heart."

"What was the attraction?"

"Truthfully?"

Robin nodded.

"At first, I think Cassandra played up to his ego, acted impressed with his military career, that sort of thing. Any man—any woman, for that matter—likes to be stroked. And Jake didn't get a lot of strokes growing up. She made him feel special. He bought right into it."

"What happened?"

"Little things. She started messing with his head, I'm not sure why. Maybe she had little control over her childhood and enjoyed manipulating Jake. Who knows."

"And they broke up because…?"

"She waited until he was gone on his second tour of duty and sent him a Dear John letter."

Robin glanced at the door to the basement. "That must have hurt."

"It did. More than it should have. I don't know what she wrote in that letter, but it caused a wound I don't think ever healed."

"Do you think he still loves her?"

"No, that's not love. It was a wish, a wish for a picture-book life with a loving woman and family. From things he said, Jake's mom's guess was that Cassandra wrote something awful in that letter about him being a horrible father because he had such a bad role model."

"But he wouldn't be a horrible father," Robin protested.

Caroline smiled. "We know that, but somewhere in Jake lies the message that because his father was an abuser, he will become one as well."

"That's ridiculous," Robin said.

"Emotional baggage isn't necessarily rooted in reality, Robin."

Like Robin's internal messages that'd she'd never be as smart as Kyle. She'd never accomplish as much as Kyle would have had he lived. *Aren't you proud of me Mama? I got an A in statistics. I'm on the debate team. I'm head of student government.*

But it was never enough in Robin's mind because all she'd heard were her mother's words: *I miss him so much.*

Yet, Robin was right there, every day, fighting to get Mom and Dad's attention.

"Robin?" Caroline questioned.

"I was just remembering some of my own baggage."

"My advice? Leave it at the door. However much you need Jake right now, he needs you more. Trust me on that."

Robin folded a bath towel. "We've only known each other a few days."

"All these rules," Caroline sighed. "The first time I met Thomas, I knew he was the one."

"How long were you married?"

"Thirty-three years. He passed away five years ago after suffering a stroke."

"I'm so sorry. I don't think I could survive the pain of losing someone like that."

Caroline touched Robin's shoulder. "We were lucky, Robin. We shared more time together than many couples do. You can't dwell on the grief. You have to celebrate the love you shared."

"I wish I could. I've been carrying the grief around since my brother died fourteen years ago."

"Would he have wanted you to carry this burden?"

"Probably not."

"Definitely not." Caroline went back to folding towels. "Nor would Thomas. Instead, I remember the laughter, the tenderness. Can you remember laughing with your brother?"

Robin smiled and remembered the day she went with him to run an errand for Mom, and how they got caught in the middle of a parade of bicycling hippies in Fremont.

"We did laugh," she paused.

"Good. Focus on that."

The rest of the afternoon flew by. Robin found herself falling into a comfortable rhythm with Caroline doing chores for the inn. It gave her a sense of peace as she shelved the dark memories of her childhood.

Robin spent the better part of her childhood wishing for Kyle to get better. Then she spent the rest trying to fill his spot in the family, by trying to make Mom and Dad doubly proud by being an overachiever, earning a degree in three and a half, not four years, and working for a foundation that helped sick kids.

Yet no matter what she did, how hard she worked to impress them, they'd drifted away, and she got the message that the wrong child had died. Why else would they push her away?

Because they focused on the grief, just like you've been doing since Kyle's death.

Well, it was time to switch gears.

Caroline, Sketch, Mack, Jake and Robin shared a delicious dinner of beef stew and biscuits. It felt like a family dinner with Sketch tossing out snarky remarks and Mack making silly-boy comments that cracked up everyone.

Robin caught Jake smiling at her, and for a second she pretended this was her real family.

And he was her husband.

She looked away, not because the fantasy frightened her, but because she couldn't ignore the fear of losing someone she loved.

There. She'd admitted it. She was falling in love with Jake, an honorable man who was a stranger just a few days ago.

Robin slept better that night than she had in months. The anxiety about her current situation drifted away. Life was sometimes hard, but things you cared about were worth the pain.

She dressed in a pair of jeans and a soft, pink T-shirt and headed downstairs for breakfast. As she passed the front room, she noticed the fire burning in the fireplace and wished she could curl up on the couch and read a book. Maybe, someday, when this was all over.

She continued toward the kitchen. The sound of Jake's voice made her pause in the hallway just outside the door.

"It's not that hard to get a GED. I'll help you study for the test if you want."

"GEDs are for losers," Sketch said.

"Who told you that?"

Sketch didn't answer.

"Well, they're wrong," Jake said. "Unless, of course, you think I'm a loser."

"You mean...you didn't graduate from high school?"

"Nope. Got my GED when I was twenty and I'm proud of it. Got my bachelor's degree when I was twenty-five."

Robin stepped into the kitchen and grabbed a mug from the rack. "What'd I miss?" she said, not wanting Jake to think she'd been eavesdropping.

"An intellectual discussion about the importance of education," Sketch said.

Robin sat at the table next to Jake. "I've got one of those. A degree, I mean."

"What kind?" Sketch said.

"Bachelor of Arts in English."

Sketch rolled his eyes.

"What? You don't think it's important to know how to communicate?" Robin challenged.

The doorbell rang, and the mood suddenly shifted.

"I'll get it," Caroline called from the front room.

Jake stood and took Robin's hand, pulling her behind the cabinets and out of sight.

And just like that, the light mood was gone, the doorbell reminding Robin that they were not a family, but strangers thrown together to defend themselves from evil.

As they hid in the corner from the unexpected visitor, Robin calmed her breathing and squeezed Jake's hand.

A few minutes later, Chief Wright came into the kitchen and glanced at Jake and Robin.

"Am I interrupting something?" He raised a brow.

"With these two?" Sketch stood and put his plate in the sink. "You're always interrupting something."

"I've got some news," Chief Wright said.

Jake released Robin and shut the kitchen door for privacy, even though Caroline's few guests had checked out yesterday.

Robin braced herself for whatever was coming next. If only she could have one unremarkable day, one day to enjoy the dream of being part of a family.

Jake's family.

"Two guys fitting the description of the men who attacked you last night were seen outside of Port Ludlow about an hour ago."

"How do you know?" Jake said.

"I've got a friend in the department. Asked him to keep an eye out."

"So, they've found us." Robin fought back the burn in her stomach.

"Not necessarily," Jake said. "They could be scouting the area."

She looked from Jake to Chief Wright.

"It's true," the chief said. "I think they would have been here by now, if they knew where you were."

"What's the plan?" Sketch said.

"The plan is, you're staying out of it," Jake said to him.

"What, because I'm seventeen?"

"Sketch, you've been a tremendous help, but I don't want to put you in danger," Jake said.

"Whatever. I'm going for a ride." Sketch marched across the kitchen and pushed open the door to the back porch.

"Wear a helmet," Jake called after him.

The door slammed, and Jake shook his head.

"That kid reminds me of someone." Chief Wright tapped his finger to his chin, and Robin caught the inference. Sketch reminded him of Jake, which was probably why Jake related to him so well.

"Anyway," the chief started. "I wouldn't worry too much. If they're on a fishing expedition they won't think to come here."

"Still, I can't risk it," Jake said.

"What are you going to do?" the chief asked.

"Maybe we should take off, find another hiding spot."

Robin's heart sank. She'd just started feeling grounded again, safe.

"I don't know if being seen in public is such a good idea. Holing up here might be smarter," the chief suggested.

Robin glanced at Jake, hopeful, but his gaze was locked on the chief's. "I don't want to put Caroline and the kids in danger, Morgan."

"There's no way they can draw a direct line to the inn, right?"

Jake thought a second, then, "Her car, it's one of a kind. We need to hide it."

"Where is it now?" Chief Wright asked.

"Behind the house."

"That thing doesn't have a garage?"

"That thing has a name," Caroline said, walking across the kitchen and putting towels in a drawer. "It's Lucy, and she understands that I need the garage for supplies."

Chief Wright put up his hands. "I stand corrected."

"You're forgiven."

"I've got room in my garage," Chief Wright said. "Drive it to my place, and I'll bring you back."

"I'll go with you." Robin stood.

Sketch raced into the kitchen out of breath. "Two guys—one's bald—just pulled in."

FIFTEEN

"Then it's a good thing I'm here," Morgan said, calmly standing.

Jake grabbed Robin and led her toward the basement door. "Stay down there until I tell you it's safe."

"What about you?"

"I'm staying up here in case Morgan needs help."

Chief Wright shot him a look.

"Morgan, these guys are killers," Jake said.

"And I'm the police. The last thing they're going to do is kill a cop. If the car's out back, there's no reason for them to suspect you're here. They're digging through the haystack, Jake. I'll redirect them and send them away."

"All the same, I'm your backup."

Jake motioned for Robin to go downstairs, but she hesitated.

"Please, Robin. You have to trust me on this." He brushed a kiss against her lips, a new, yet automatic, response.

"You come get me the minute they leave," she said.

"Sketch, go down there with her," Jake ordered.

The kid accompanied her into the basement.

"I don't want Caroline answering the door," Jake said. "I don't want her anywhere near them."

"They won't even get in the house," Morgan said.

"Caroline, stay in the kitchen," Jake said.

"No, wait, I've got a better idea," Morgan said. He led Caroline to the front of the house, whispering instructions. Jake didn't like involving her but trusted Morgan's instincts.

Hoping to listen in on the conversation through the open window, Jake hid behind the grandfather clock in the sitting room.

He waited five minutes, maybe ten. But nothing happened. He peeked through the window sheers and spotted the men walking up to the house.

Jake ducked behind the clock, out of sight, and held his breath.

"Thank you very much Mrs. Ross," Morgan said.

"My pleasure Chief Wright." Caroline shut the front door and walked back into the kitchen.

"Officer?" One of the men greeted him.

"Good morning," Morgan said. "I see you've found the best inn on the peninsula."

"It came highly recommended."

Oh, no. If they booked a room here…

"Is there something we should know about?" the man said. "I mean, if a police officer is here…"

"I was following up on a missing person's bulletin."

"Who's missing?" the second man said.

"A couple from Seattle. The innkeeper said she thinks they stayed here last night, but you know small towns. Everyone's looking for drama."

"Are they dangerous?" Death Eyes said.

"Could be. But they're long gone by now. They left this morning."

"That's unfortunate for the police, huh?" the stocky guy said.

"Not really. I just got a call they were spotted in Sequim about twenty minutes ago." Morgan paused. "When are these criminals going to realize they can't hide from the police?"

Jake held his breath. *Don't push it, Morgan.*

"Anyway, the inn has the best scones in town, plus afternoon tea with award-winning cookies."

Morgan, back off. You don't want to sell them on staying here.

"Actually, we were looking for something closer to the water." The second guy said.

"Well, there's the Blue Goose Motel on Front Street, Cooper's Cottage and The Sleepy Eagle."

Three sets of footsteps clomped down the front stairs. Morgan's voice got softer as he and the men wandered to their cars.

"They're all down by the Town Center. I can show you, if you'd like."

"No, that's okay," Death Eyes said. "We'll find it. Thanks, sheriff."

"Chief."

"Right. Sorry."

Car engines started up and Jake counted to twenty. They were surely gone by now, right?

But he still couldn't move. The men who were after Robin had been within spitting distance from Jake, and he'd been unable to do a thing about it other than wait it out and trust Morgan to handle the situation. Which he had done quite well.

Jake peeked through the sheers and spotted the dark sedan turning onto Chestnut with Morgan's car close behind. Jake spotted Sketch take off on his bike.

In the same direction as the sedan.

"Sketch," Jake said under his breath.

The ringing phone distracted him, and Caroline came into the front room. "It's Morgan."

Jake took the phone. "You are a master, my friend."

"You're welcome."

"The kid, Sketch, took off after them."

"Why would he do that?"

"I don't know. Maybe he wasn't really after them. Maybe he was just going for a joy ride."

"I'll keep an eye out for him. I'm going to alert a friend who runs the garage on the outskirts of town to be on the lookout for their sedan. Once they leave Port Whisper, you should be okay."

"Thanks to your wild goose chase."

"Ah, how I love tricking the enemy. I'll check in later."

Jake went into the kitchen and opened the basement door. "Robin?"

She didn't answer, and his blood pressure spiked. He rushed downstairs and froze at the sight of Robin, hands folded together and eyes closed. She was whispering something under her breath.

"Robin?" he said again.

She glanced up. "It helped, it really helped."

"What helped?"

"Praying." She stood and wandered closer to him. "It calmed me down, so I didn't completely freak out down here."

"I'm glad. Where's Sketch?"

"He took off. What happened?"

"Morgan told the men we headed west. They left to pick up the trail." He led her upstairs to the kitchen where Caroline was brewing tea.

"But they could come back," Robin said.

"Unlikely," he said to calm her, knowing full well anything was possible.

"My hands are still shaking," Robin said.

"I don't know about you two, but I could use a cup of tea," Caroline said.

Jake glanced at Robin. "Caroline's remedy for everything."

"It works," Caroline shot back.

They were all trying to ease the adrenaline rush and put the tense few minutes behind them. Robin sat at the kitchen table.

"I don't like sitting here, waiting for something to happen.

Can't Detective Beck do something with that sketch we sent him?"

"I'm sure he's working on it."

"I wish I had something to hold on to, something to give me hope," she said.

Jake leaned forward, squeezed her hand between his and smiled. He didn't need to say anything. He could tell from her eyes that she understood his silent communication. *Hold on to me.*

He realized he needed the connection as much as she did.

The back door burst open, and an excited Mack raced into the kitchen. "We climbed the Monster Tree!" he shouted running to Caroline and hugging her legs. She chuckled and rubbed his back.

And just like that, the tension was gone.

A teenage girl followed Mack into the kitchen. She had fair skin with freckles and red hair tied back in a ponytail.

"Jake, Robin, this is Ashley Rubin," Caroline introduced.

"Ah, you're the couple Sketch's been talking about," Ashley said.

Before Jake could respond, Robin stepped in. "What's that stinker been saying?"

"Oh, nothing," she said with a smile. She glanced through the front hallway. "Is Sketch…home?"

"No, sorry," Jake said.

"Oh," she said with a disappointed frown. "Well, tell him I said hi."

"I will, honey," Caroline said. "Thanks for taking Mack on an adventure."

"Sure, he's a great kid. Well, see ya." Ashley bounced out the back door.

The inn's phone rang, and Caroline picked it up. "Port Whisper Inn. Hey, Morgan." She glanced at Jake. "Sure." She handed Jake the phone.

"What's up?" Jake said.

"My mechanic buddy spotted the sedan speeding out of town. Wish I'd been there to give them a ticket."

"I'm glad you weren't."

"Gee, thanks. I think. Anyway, you guys should be good for another couple of days. What's the word from Ethan?"

"Nothing today. I'll keep you posted."

"You do that. I can only help you if you let me know what's going on."

"Understood." Jake handed Caroline the phone. "Looks like Morgan worked his magic. Their car was spotted leaving town."

Robin breathed a sigh of relief. "So, what now?"

"I'm redecorating the Rainier Room upstairs," Caroline said. "If you want to help, that would be great."

Robin glanced at Jake.

"Wouldn't be a bad idea to keep your mind off things," he offered.

Caroline narrowed her eyes at Jake. "You might not say that when I give you your assignment, young man."

By the end of the day, Jake had covered two-thirds of a honey-do list Caroline had given him. He'd wander upstairs every hour to check on Robin, Caroline would ask how he was doing on the list and then he'd head back downstairs. He couldn't help it. He was only convinced that Robin was okay if he saw her with his own eyes.

Pumped with enthusiasm for the redecorating project, Robin looked energized and beautiful. It amazed him how she could compartmentalize her fear of being stalked and focus on the task at hand. She was better at it than Jake, that's for sure. He still fought to silence Death Eyes's threat from the other night.

We're going to use her feelings for you to get her back...and kill her.

But Jake would make sure no one got close enough to hurt Robin. He'd protect her for as long as necessary. Even forever.

No doubt about it. He was a goner.

Jake drilled a hinge into a kitchen cabinet, which had been loose. It felt good to be useful like this, to work with his hands. Yet, a part of his head was buzzing with strategy for saving Robin.

He stood and went to the sink for a glass of water.

The back door burst open, slamming against the wall. Sketch rushed to the kitchen table and whipped out his laptop from his backpack.

"Where have you been?" Jake said. "Your girl was looking for you."

"Never mind about that. You need to see this." He tapped on his keyboard and a news site came up. "I was searching Seattle police stories and came across this. Happened earlier today and just hit the news sites."

Jake read the opening sentence, and the air rushed from his lungs.

Seattle Police Officer Ethan Beck and two other motorists were seriously injured in a three-car collision on Alaskan Way.

"Ethan. No," Jake breathed.

"There's more. They're saying it's drug-related."

"Drug-related, how?"

Sketch pointed to the screen and read. "Police suspect Detective Ethan Beck was under the influence of a narcotic which caused him to lose control of his vehicle."

SIXTEEN

Jake slammed his water glass on the table. "Ethan's never done a drug in his life."

"Well, something made him swerve into another lane," Sketch said. "He's at Harborview. I could break into the hospital's system and find out—"

"No. No breaking into anything." Without thinking, he grabbed the wall phone. "I'll call the hospital to find out his status."

"No!" Sketch ripped the phone out of Jake's hand. "You can't use the landline."

Jake glanced at the teenager and realized the kid was thinking with a clear head, while Jake was charged by anger. Ethan didn't take drugs. Once they'd practically had to shove a painkiller down his throat when he'd taken shrapnel in the leg.

Which meant this was a setup. Someone had intentionally drugged Ethan.

Jake could barely see past the frustration blinding him. Ethan was a good man, doing a hard job, and didn't know who to trust in his department. And now, he was in the hospital fighting for his life.

"I should go see him," Jake muttered.

"See who?" Robin said, wandering into the kitchen. She read his expression and stopped short. "What?"

"Ethan was in a car accident. He's in the hospital and I don't know how bad it is."

"Jake I'm so sorry." She reached out, but he stepped away and paced the kitchen, trying to think clearly enough to strategize his next move.

"Kid, can I use your untraceable phone?" he asked.

"I'm on it." Sketch rushed downstairs.

"What do you think happened?" Robin said.

"He didn't abuse drugs. I can guarantee that."

"Is that what they're saying?" She crossed her arms over her chest and leaned against the counter.

"Yeah, which is ridiculous, especially since the department would normally do their best to keep something like that quiet until they knew for sure."

"Which means this is coming from inside the department."

"Which Ethan suspected from the get-go."

Sketch came back into the kitchen with the phone.

"Can you find me the number for Harborview?" Jake asked Sketch.

"They won't tell you anything, not over the phone," Sketch said. "When Dad was taken to the hospital, Mom wouldn't let me go so I called, told them I was his son, but they wouldn't tell me anything other than he was there. Calling the hospital's a waste of time."

"I've got to know he's going to be okay," Jake said, struggling to clear his head.

"Has he got a wife or something? Call her," Sketch offered.

"No, but he's got three older brothers. Alex is an attorney in Seattle. Ethan was going to talk to him about the case. Can you track him down?"

"Yep." Sketch sat at the kitchen table and punched away at his laptop. "Got any idea how old he is, or where he grew up?"

"I'm guessing he's thirty-four. They grew up in Seattle—Ballard neighborhood—with me."

"Good, give me a minute."

Jake continued his frantic pacing, trying to figure out what to do next other than rush back to Seattle and sit beside his friend's hospital bed. No, Ethan would be furious with Jake if he jeopardized the case by exposing his whereabouts. Because if they found Jake, they had access to Robin, and whoever was behind all this would have the ace card.

Somehow, some way, they'd work on Jake until he revealed where she was. Yeah, he'd be dead before he uttered a word, and he was no good to Robin dead.

"Jake?" Robin caught up to him and took his hand. "He'll be okay. He's a strong man, and very determined."

Jake shrugged, brushing his thumb across the back of her hand. "I don't know how to help him."

"Yes, you do. Protect me, and put the jerks behind all this in jail. I'm guessing Detective Beck was close to finding out the truth about who's behind the killing and drug smuggling, and that's why he's in the hospital."

"I can't believe one of his own men drugged him."

"There are bad people everywhere. I'm sorry your friend got caught up in this mess."

Jake pulled her to his chest in a hug. "Right. You're sorry about Ethan even though your life's been in danger for days." He broke the embrace and tipped her chin up to look into her eyes. "You are a remarkable woman, Robin."

"Gag me." Sketch rolled his eyes. "If you two are done, I've got the brother's phone number."

Sketch handed Jake the phone. "Remember, it's untraceable if you call, but if you give the number out, I can't guarantee they won't find you."

With a nod, Jake punched in the number. It rang once, twice. If Alex didn't answer should Jake risk leaving a message?

"Hello?"

Relief washed over Jake. "Alex?"

"Yes."

"It's Jake Walters. I heard about Ethan."

"He'll understand, Aunt Gert. Don't worry about it."

"You're not alone. I get it. Did you know Ethan was working on something involving police corruption?"

"Didn't you get the email? It's better if you stay home."

"We need to talk, Alex. When can I call you?"

"We won't know until later tonight. Nine, ten, something like that."

"I'll call you back. Just tell me he's going to be okay."

A pregnant pause and then, "We don't know yet."

Jake closed his eyes. "Alex, I'm so sorry."

"Thanks for the call, Aunt Gert," he said in soft, broken voice. "Bye."

Alex hung up and Jake stared at the phone. His best friend was in critical condition, and Jake couldn't do a thing about it. He couldn't support the family, pray with them, keep a vigil at the hospital. All he could do was stay away and hope for the best.

"It's bad?" Robin asked.

"Sounds like. He couldn't talk. Someone was there." A bad guy, a villain. Jake prayed some of the good folks showed up as well to support Ethan: friends from church, family and neighbors. Jake hated feeling helpless. He'd felt helpless growing up, helpless for the months he'd taken care of Mom, and had watched the life dim in her eyes.

With a burst of frustration, he slammed his fist on the kitchen table, then glanced up at Robin, fearing her reaction. But Robin didn't flinch, step back or look frightened in the least.

"Feel better?" she said.

"I usually do," Sketch muttered. "I've got a punching bag in the basement if you want to go a few rounds with that."

"Thanks for the offer," Jake said. "Hey, Alex said something about an email. It might have been a smoke screen, but then again, maybe Ethan sent me something before the accident."

Yeah, and who was Jake going to take it to? At this point, he couldn't trust anyone in the department.

Jake spotted an email sent from Ethan's personal account. With Robin looking over his shoulder and Sketch sitting next to him, Jake clicked it open.

Jake,

Attached are copies of documents I found in Detective Edwards's lock box. I'm sending my brother, Alex, copies as well. He trusts someone in the district attorney's office and is going to pursue that angle.

I think someone broke into my place looking for it, so I'm keeping it in the trunk of my car.

On my way to speak with the police chief—under the radar, of course. Who knows how far up this goes, but I have to do something.

Thanks,

E

Jake downloaded four attachments and saved them to the desktop. He signed off quickly.

"Do you think they can trace us now that I've checked my email?" he asked Sketch.

"Depends on how frequently they're checking his and your email accounts."

"Okay, let's look at this stuff." He glanced over his shoulder at Robin. "Ready?"

"Yes, sir."

"Well, I'm ready for some dinner," Caroline said, breezing into the kitchen. "What's so fascinating on the computer?"

"An email from Ethan from this morning," Jake said. "He was in a car accident this afternoon."

"Oh no," she sighed.

"Jake thinks Ethan was drugged," Robin said.

"But they set it up to look like it was his fault," Sketch added.

"Which is why I'm going to figure out how to put an end to this." He clicked on one of the documents, and a shipping manifest popped onto the screen. "I'm going to build a case, clear Ethan's name and get Robin's life back for her."

"Okay, superhero, what do you need me to do?" Sketch said.

"Help me figure out how to sneak back into Seattle under the radar."

"You think that's a good idea?" Caroline said.

"I do. They won't be expecting it. They expect us to hide and keep running. If there's one thing I can't stand, it's bullies."

"No kidding," Sketch said.

"I'll whip something up for dinner," Caroline said. "Robin, would you like to help?"

"Of course."

"We should take this downstairs. My other computer is faster," Sketch said.

Sketch packed up the laptop and headed downstairs. Jake went to Robin, who was taking down plates for dinner.

"We're going to end this and get your life back." He automatically kissed her.

She shot him a half smile. "Thanks."

For the next hour, Robin helped Caroline prepare dinner. Sadness crept into her thoughts, sadness about Detective Beck, sadness about the police corruption. Sadness that when this was over, her relationship with Jake would end as well.

Caroline touched Robin's shoulder. "It will be okay. Jake won't let anything happen to you."

"I know."

"Then, what is it?"

Robin shook her head.

"He truly cares about you, Robin. Don't let him tell you otherwise."

"Why would he fight it?"

"Perhaps because he hasn't had such great experiences with women, perhaps because he's afraid he'd be a bad father," Robin said.

"We both know that's ridiculous. Look how he is with Sketch and little Mack."

"It's odd, I know, but sometimes we believe things others say about us, even if they're untrue."

Like Robin believing it when her parents said it was okay that she wasn't as smart or as talented as her older brother.

"Like Jake's ex-girlfriend telling him he'd be a bad father," Robin said.

"Yes, but never mind that."

Chief Wright tapped on the back door and waved at Robin through the glass. She let him in.

"Ladies," he said with a smile.

"Morgan, did you smell my fried chicken all the way down the block?" Caroline said.

"I wish my motivation was strictly hunger pangs. I need to speak with Jake."

"They're downstairs," Robin offered.

As Chief Wright headed downstairs, the phone rang, and a timer went off.

"You pull the chicken out, and I'll answer the phone," Caroline said.

Robin did as ordered, pulled the chicken out of the oven and searched for serving utensils.

"Port Whisper Inn," Caroline answered.

"Pardon me? Slow down.… Who? Robin Strand?"

Robin snapped her attention to Caroline.

"No, she's not a guest. I'm sorry I can't help you Jennifer. If she does check in I'll be sure to—"

Robin snatched the phone from Caroline. "Hello?"

"Robin, I'm so glad I found you," Jenn said.

"How did you get this number?"

"Detective Beck," Jenn said. "Listen, the retirement village left messages on your work phone about your dad. He's in the hospital. They think it's a stroke."

"What hospital?"

"St. Joseph's in Phoenix. I'm sorry I didn't reach you sooner, but I didn't know where you were, and I panicked and finally convinced Detective Beck to give me the number and—"

"Thanks, Jenn. I've got to go."

"But—"

Robin hung up and dialed four-one-one. "I have to call information, Caroline. I'll pay you back."

Feeling unusually calm, Robin called information and got the number for the hospital.

The men came upstairs into the kitchen, Jake looking at Robin with question in his eyes.

"Her father had a stroke," Caroline said.

"How does she know that?" Jake said.

"Her friend, Jenn, called," Caroline explained.

"Directory Assistance," the voice said.

"I need a number in Phoenix for St. Joseph's Hospital." Robin scribbled the number on the message board by the phone.

"Thanks," she said to the operator and hung up.

"How did Jenn find us?" Jake asked.

"Detective Beck," Robin explained dialing the hospital.

"No, use the Batphone." Sketch handed it to her. She called the hospital and sensed whispering behind her but did her best to shut it out.

"St. Joseph's Hospital."

"Hi, my name is Robin Strand, and I'm calling about my father, William, who was brought in today."

"Please hold."

Robin glanced at Jake, who motioned to Caroline. She nodded and rushed past Robin into the front hallway and up the stairs. Robin wasn't sure what was going on and didn't care. She needed to find out if Dad was okay.

A moment later the operator came back on the line. "I'm

sorry, we don't have a patient by that name registered at the hospital."

"But… Are you sure? Can you check again?"

"William Strand was not admitted. I'm sorry ma'am."

Robin hung up and handed the phone to Sketch. "I don't understand. Jenn said he was at St. Joseph's."

Jake placed both hands on her shoulders, calming her anxiety. "Robin, we should consider the possibility that this is part of their plan."

"Giving my dad a stroke?"

"No, but by leaving that message and having Jenn track you down, they could pin down our exact location."

"It isn't always about this case, Jake. My father could be dying, and I can't get to him."

Jake pulled her against his chest, and she held on, fearing that she'd never see Dad again. She and her parents weren't all that close, but what she'd been through these past few days, coupled with the thought of losing him, made her want to remedy that relationship.

She somehow had grown to understand them better, realized that she had been doing the same thing, keeping loved ones at arm's length for fear of losing them and having to survive the pain.

Like they all felt when Kyle passed away.

"Can you call your mom?" Chief Wright offered.

"Good idea." Jake got the number and Sketch handed her the phone. Unfortunately the call went into voice mail.

Caroline came downstairs with the backpack they'd bought for Robin's new things. "You're ready to go."

"What, now?" Robin said.

"I'll pack up some dinner for you to take on the road." Caroline pulled out containers.

"There's a ferry leaving at eleven-fifteen," Jake said. "We can make that one. I'm going to pack. You—" Jake pointed at Chief Wright "—keep an eye on her."

"You think they'll come back?" Robin said.

"I don't know," Jake said. "But the fact that your friend found us concerns me."

"She said Detective Beck gave her the number."

"Not likely. Let's discuss this later, okay? Morgan, which car did you drive?"

"My off-duty pickup."

"Interested in a trade? Just for a few days."

"Sure, if I'm trading up," he joked.

Robin couldn't believe how the chief could have a sense of humor with all this tension filling the room.

"I'll put this in the pickup." Chief Wright took Robin's pack and headed outside.

"Relax for a second." Caroline encouraged Robin to sit at the table. "Jake's right. It's probably just a trick to get you out of hiding."

"Which means they're coming back here, putting you and your family in danger. Oh, Caroline, I'm so sorry."

"Stop. Morgan loves my cooking. He'll camp out and keep watch over us tonight. Then again, maybe we'll all camp out in Morgan's living room while he watches over the house."

"I have to talk to my dad," Robin said.

"You're all set," Chief Wright said, stepping into the kitchen.

Jake bounded down the stairs and rushed into the kitchen as well. "Okay, let's go."

Sketch put out his fist, and Jake bumped it with his own. "Stay out of trouble," Jake said. The kid smiled. Robin hugged Caroline.

"Thanks, for everything," Robin said from the back door.

Jake led her to the truck and they took off. Robin glanced through the back window at the house, so charming, full of love and hope.

And, at that moment, she knew what she'd been missing

her whole life: the feeling of family and love that completed a person's soul.

"You okay?" Jake said.

"Yeah." She opened a container, and the aroma of fried chicken made her mouth water. "With everything that's going on, I can't believe I'm even hungry."

"It's Caroline's cooking."

She glanced at Jake. His eyes were constantly scanning the road, the rearview mirror, and the side mirrors. He was on alert, ready to fight.

"See anything?" she said.

"Nope." He shot her a smile.

"Good, then have something to eat." She forked a piece of chicken and held it to his lips.

He chewed and rolled his eyes. "Man, that woman can cook."

"Jake?"

"Yeah?"

"Do you really think my dad's stroke could be a lie?"

"Yes, I do. Look, you wouldn't be doing anything differently if he were in the hospital than you are right now."

"True." She leaned back and prayed for another chance with her folks.

The ride to the ferry landing went quicker than Jake thought, especially considering his body was still strung tight with tension. Robin surprised him, trying to take the tension out of the air by chatting about Caroline and her family. He knew she was masking utter panic about her father.

The whole thing felt off: her father's stroke, not being able to locate him at the hospital and even Ethan giving Robin's friend the inn's number in the first place. Jake doubted it was Ethan who gave Jenn the number, which meant whoever was behind this might have tracked them.

He clenched his jaw at the thought of the two men returning

to The Port Whisper Inn looking for Jake and Robin. He hoped Morgan was able to talk Caroline and the kids into a sleepover at his house. Jake had a feeling Sketch wouldn't want to leave his master command center in the basement.

"What's the plan when we get to Seattle?" Robin asked as Jake pulled onto the ferry.

"Find Alex, Ethan's brother. Check on the status of the case, find out how Ethan's doing."

"All while being invisible. Great."

"Hey, at first glance I doubt anyone would recognize you with the blond hair and glasses."

"Death Eyes and his partner will. They saw me at the ferry landing the other night, remember?"

"Then we'll be careful to avoid them. I just wish we knew who to trust in the P.D."

Jake kept checking the cars behind him but didn't see anything suspicious. Besides, if Jenn's call was part of a strategy to locate Jake and Robin it would take Death Eyes and his partner time to get back to the inn.

He and Robin should be safe, for now.

"It's probably best if we stay in the car," Jake said, glancing at a man and woman getting out of the car next to them. "I'm going to give Alex a call."

Jake called Ethan's brother from a disposable phone he'd bought on the way to the ferry and he picked up on the first ring. "Alex Beck."

"Alex, it's Jake."

"Great, I've been waiting to hear from you. Where are you?"

"On the way back. How's Ethan?"

"Stable. That's the good news. Jake, they're investigating him. They suspect he was involved with the drug ring."

"That's ridiculous."

"No kidding. The best thing we've got going for us is Robin Strand, the witness. Is she with you?"

"Yes."

"The second man she saw that night is the key. This is big, Jake. Ethan was on his way to meet with the chief and show him the sketch you sent when he was in the accident."

"What can I do?"

"We need to meet. Stash Robin someplace safe. But don't talk about it over the phone."

"I've got a throwaway cell."

"I wouldn't be surprised if they tapped mine. Remember where we used to go for church picnics when we were kids?"

"Yep."

"Can you meet me there in, say, an hour?"

Jake did the math in his head. "Shouldn't be a problem."

"Jake?" Robin gripped his arm. "Look."

He glanced in the rearview mirror and spotted two men going from car to car, shining a flashlight into empty cars.

Death Eyes and his partner.

SEVENTEEN

Robin's heart was pounding as Jake motioned for her to exit the car on her side. Jake followed her and whispered, "Stay low."

They practically crawled around the corner to the other section of cars.

"We need to keep moving." He pulled her to the other side of the ferry and crouched beside a van.

"How did they find us?"

"Doesn't matter." He led her down the aisle behind a compact car. He peered around the corner. "They've split up."

He glanced at surrounding cars and pulled her behind him to a Suburban. "Get under here, quickly."

She shimmied beneath the truck and held her breath. "Jake?" she whispered.

"They're headed this way. I need to divert them."

"No." Her voice was hushed, but he was gone.

Anxiety screamed in her head that she might never see Jake again, and her pulse raced triple-time. She wanted to rush out and follow him, stay close to him.

But having an anxiety attack and exposing her location would only put Jake in danger. He must have a plan, right? A plan to divert the men from Robin's location? But what if his plan didn't work, what if the men got their hands on Jake like before?

What if they killed him?

A gut-wrenching ache clawed its way up her chest—an old,

familiar ache she wished she could bury once and for all. But it was always with her.

The devastating ache of loss. It shot across her nerve endings to her fingertips. She couldn't lose Jake, after just having found him, this special man who had taught her to open her heart to God. He was a strong yet vulnerable man who she couldn't imagine living without…

She closed her eyes, focused on prayer, but instead of praying for strength, she found herself praying for Jake.

I'll do anything, God, if You'd save Jake's life.

Please, God. Please.

She clasped her hands together, squeezed her eyes shut and whispered the prayer over and over again.

I love him, Lord. Please save him. He doesn't deserve to die because of me.

"Hey! Over there!" a man shouted.

She choked back a gasp and pictured the men spotting Jake, chasing him…

Tossing him over the side of the ferry.

She loved Jake and was willing to do anything to save his life, even if that meant letting him go.

Please, Lord, I'll walk away from Jake if You'd save him. It's my fault he's in danger. Please save him.

Minutes passed like hours as she lay there, picturing the attack. But no, they wouldn't kill Jake, not until they found Robin. The best thing she could do—besides pray for his life—was stay put and stay safe. As long as they didn't know where she was, Jake had a chance.

She took a slow, deep breath, then another. She must have been lying there for twenty minutes when the engines slowed. They were approaching the dock. A new wave of panic settled deep in her chest. What would she do when they disembarked?

"Robin?" Jake whispered.

She snapped her gaze to her left and saw Jake's gorgeous blue-green eyes looking at her.

"Let's go." He motioned for her to crawl out from under the truck.

"What happened?" she said, elated that Jake was alive.

"I neutralized them."

With a comforting hand, he led her to the car. He was alive; he was okay.

Please, Lord, I'll walk away from Jake if You'll save him.

She'd made a promise, just as Jake had made one at the hospital when he said he would protect her. Somehow—she wasn't sure how—she was going to keep her promise.

"Ethan's brother will help us," Jake said, hoping to comfort Robin. She'd been strangely quiet since the threat on the ferry, didn't ask about what had happened or how Jake had neutralized the men.

It had been relatively easy, since they'd separated to carry out their search. He took them down one at a time. He'd shoved the stocky guy into a closet and Death Eyes into his car, binding his hands with duct tape Jake had found in Morgan's truck.

Jake had been able to bury his feelings for Robin so he could focus on treating this like an official mission to take down the enemy.

"You okay?" he asked, wishing he could read her thoughts.

"May I call my Mom's cell again?"

"Sure." He pulled his throwaway cell from his pocket and handed it to her but noticed she wouldn't look at him. Was she horrified that he'd used violence to neutralize the men? Or was she still in shock over what had just happened?

As they headed north toward the park in Ballard, he kept checking his rearview mirror. He didn't spot the sedan. Ferry workers probably had found Death Eyes, gagged and bound in his car, and then he'd spun some wild tale about being attacked on the ferry.

Whatever he did was irrelevant. They'd gotten away, and

Jake had to focus on the next step in this mission: meeting up with Alex.

"Mom?" Robin sat straight. "No everything's fine I just… How's dad?… Daddy, are you okay?"

Robin slumped back against the seat and closed her eyes. "I'm sorry. I know it's late….No, I had a nightmare and had to call. Sure… No, no, go back to sleep. I'll be fine. I just…miss you…. Uh-huh…. Okay, that sounds great…. Love you, too."

She closed the phone and a choke-gasp escaped her lips. "He's okay, everyone's okay. He's not in the hospital. They're at home, and I woke them up."

He reached out and touched her hair, but she didn't lean into his touch like she had back at the inn. He slipped his hand to the steering wheel. "That's great news."

"It was all a lie to get me to come back?" she said. "Which means they're using Jenn to get to me."

"It'll be over soon," Jake offered.

She looked at him with a sad smile. "Yes, it will. And before I forget, I want to say, thanks, truly, for everything you've done for me."

He didn't like the sound of that. He wanted to press her on what she meant, but his cell rang. He'd only given the number to Morgan and Caroline. He nodded for her to answer since he was driving.

"Hello…? Alex?" She looked at Jake.

Jake pulled into a gas station parking lot and she handed him the phone.

"How's Ethan?" Jake said, fearing the answer.

"He's better, actually. Broken leg, minor contusions, but he didn't mess up any internal organs, so we're hopeful he'll make a full recovery."

"That's great news. How did you get this number?"

"Called the inn. Listen, we can't meet tonight. I'm being fol-lowed. I've got a better idea. The police chief's going to be at a press conference at city hall tomorrow morning at nine. I'll show up with the documentation and present it to him."

"Present what, exactly?"

"Evidence about the drug smuggling and the fact that someone on the police force was being paid to look the other way. Detective Edwards uncovered solid proof but couldn't identify who was the top dog."

"You think it's the chief?"

"No, he's a good man. Let's just hope I can convince him that Ethan wasn't involved."

"I'll meet you at city hall tomorrow."

"I'm not sure that's a good idea. They could arrest you on bogus charges."

"I need to see this through to the end, Alex."

"Your call. What about the woman?"

"I'll stash her someplace safe."

"Good. See you tomorrow."

"You take care of yourself."

"Don't worry about me. I'm headed to my brother's. He's a security expert. Maybe I'll bring him tomorrow as my bodyguard."

"Smart man."

"Some days. Take care, buddy."

"You, too."

Jake pocketed the phone and leaned back against the car seat, thanking God that Ethan would be okay.

"Jake?" Robin said.

He glanced at her and smiled. "Looks like Ethan's going to be okay."

"That's wonderful." She unbuckled her seat belt and leaned over to hug him.

He held her close, inhaling the floral scent of her hair, and sighed with relief.

Robin broke the embrace rather quickly and looked away. Something was definitely wrong.

"Are we still meeting him tonight?" she said.

"No. Alex was being followed. We'll find a place to spend the night, and I'll meet him at city hall tomorrow at nine. The police chief's going to be there for a press conference. We'll present him with the evidence then."

"Oh, okay."

He half expected her to fight him on this, argue that she needed to go with him, but she didn't.

Jake made a call to the Mar Queen Hotel and found them a room. Actually, he found Robin a room. He'd sit it out in the lobby, keeping watch for his enemies.

Even though they'd lost their pursuers, he wouldn't risk them tracking down Robin.

Half an hour later, Jake escorted Robin to her room.

She wandered through the sitting area and kitchen. Most of the rooms had separate bedrooms and kitchenettes and Jake thought it would be more comfortable than a basic hotel room. Plus, if she could make her own food she wouldn't have to leave.

"It should only be one night," Jake said. "Hopefully, we'll clear this up tomorrow morning."

She nodded, but didn't look at him.

"Robin, what is it?"

"I just want it to be over."

"Yeah, I know." He stepped toward her, but she wrapped her arms around her midsection and glanced at the floor. It didn't take a genius to read that body language. "Okay. Well, I'll be down the hall in the lobby."

"You're not staying in a room?"

"I can watch things better from the lobby."

"You think they'll find us?"

"No, but I can't afford to let my guard down. So," he hesitated, "sweet dreams."

"Thanks." Again, no eye contact.

Jake left the room and pulled on the door handle to make sure it was secure. Wandering to the lobby, he fought back his concern about Robin's mood and focused on hope. Hope that they'd wrap this up tomorrow, and they could both get on with their safe and uneventful lives.

Together.

Jake flopped down on the couch and wondered how open Robin would be to going on a date with him after this was all over. Yet, he'd been the one since the beginning to keep her at a distance, telling her this was about transference, not true emotion.

But, in the past few days, he'd grown to realize that was bogus. Jake had genuine and deep feelings for the woman who could live on Market donuts. He eyed the hallway and wondered if she'd consider the possibility of a future together or if being around him would only remind her of many near-death experiences.

It didn't matter. After the case was over and the real suspects arrested, Jake was going to reach out to Robin in the hopes they could be more than strangers on the run.

"I checked on Caroline and the kids. They're all okay," Jake said the next morning when he stopped by to check on Robin.

"I'm so glad."

"Okay, you know the drill. Stay here, and stay safe," Jake ordered.

"Where would I go?" she said.

"Robin?" He reached out to take her hand, but she grabbed her tea and cradled the cup with both hands. She couldn't take much more of this—his compassion, his caring—when she knew she'd be without it after today.

"I don't know what's going on, but, when this is over we're going to talk, okay?" he said.

He tipped her chin up with his forefinger and thumb and kissed her. She welcomed her last kiss from this man and lost herself in the moment. It was sweet and tender, and she struggled to fight back tears. She wouldn't cry. She'd be brave, as he had been, and keep her promise.

Jake hesitated in the doorway and shot her a smile meant to comfort. But it didn't. It just reminded her of what she'd be missing.

The door clicked shut, and she wandered to the sofa and sat down. It would be over soon. Jake and Alex would help police unravel this case, and she'd get her life back.

Her workaholic life.

"Can hardly wait," she whispered.

Things had shifted in Robin's world. They'd never be the same. The things that had motivated her before—like trying to impress her parents by devoting herself to raising money for children's causes—had drifted away. Being so close to death so many times made her take stock of everything, forcing her to ask the question, what do I really want.

She closed her eyes and sighed. Yes, she loved her work, but, in the past few days, she'd also opened up to something more....

Love and family.

That's when she'd realized she'd been burying herself in work to avoid confronting her pain. Wasn't it about time she moved on? Yes, she was ready. If only she could move on with Jake.

She poured another cup of tea and flipped on the television. The morning program cut to the scene of the press conference.

"Good morning," the police chief started. "As you know, we've lost two of our officers in the past seventy-two hours, first at the Chambers Building, then in Greenlake." The chief glanced into the audience at someone, then looked directly at the camera. "Our detectives are doing everything in their power to solve these cases and dispel any suspicion of police corruption."

"Chief Burns," a man interrupted. The camera panned to Mayoral Candidate Rockwell. "Don't you think it would be wise to enlist the help of an external agency to continue the investigation?"

"No, I don't. We're already making progress and should have a solid case by the end of the week." As Chief Burns continued speaking, the camera focused on Candidate Rockwell for a reaction. A man, perhaps his assistant, whispered something in the candidate's ear, and stepped back…

"No way." Robin sat up straight.

The second man at the shooting!

Robin jumped up and frantically paced the room. If Rockwell's assistant was involved in the shooting, could he have been taking orders from Rockwell himself? The same man who made it his life's purpose to expose police corruption?

Jake said police were investigating Remmington Imports and the entire police force, but what if this was all a diversion from the guy who was truly guilty?

She had to get to Jake, give him this piece of information to share with the chief, but she had no money to take a cab, city hall was at the south end of town, while the hotel was at the north. She couldn't walk. She needed help.

She picked up the hotel phone and dialed.

"Hello?" Jenn answered.

"Jenn, it's Robin. It's an emergency."

As Jenn zipped down Fifth Avenue, Robin's pulse tapped against her throat.

"I thought this was about police corruption," Jenn said.

"I'm not sure what it's about, but I know I saw Rockwell's assistant at the shooting."

"Why would he be there? Rockwell is like Mr. Clean-up-the-city, all-around great guy."

"Maybe he isn't. Things aren't always what they appear to be, Jenn."

"Hang on, I'm getting a call." Jenn pressed her earpiece and answered. "This is Jenn. Yep, on my way."

Jenn hung up and sighed. "Sorry, work."

"I don't want to get you into trouble," Robin offered.

"You're not. It's okay. Help me scout for parking."

"No. Drop me off."

"No can do. There." Jenn pointed to an empty spot in a lot.

They parked and raced to city hall where the conference was being held outside due to the large crowd.

"Let's try this corner. We can see better." Jenn led Robin to the edge of the crowd.

"I need to find Jake," Robin said, straining to see over a tall man in front of her. She scanned the crowd and spotted Jake standing near the front with another man, probably Alex. "There!"

She started through the crowd when someone grabbed her arm. She spun around and looked up into Death Eyes's sinister face.

"I knew you'd show up."

EIGHTEEN

Every nerve ending in her body screamed with panic.

"Thanks," Death Eyes said to Jenn.

Robin snapped her focus to her friend.

"I don't understand," Robin said.

"You shouldn't have been at the office, Robin," Jenn said. "I'm sorry."

She turned and walked away. Confused and devastated, Robin stared at her.

"Come on," Death Eyes said.

Robin started to call out to Jake, but Death Eyes squeezed her arm. Tight. "Do it, and your boy is dead."

She glanced across the crowd and spotted Detective Dunn standing behind Jake holding something at a right angle in his hand. A gun?

"He's not going to shoot him in public," Robin said.

"No, but he'll inject him with an overdose that'll put him in a coma. It's a great new drug we've discovered."

No. She couldn't lose Jake this way, not after everything they'd endured.

Not after they'd fallen in love.

"Let's go."

As he pulled Robin away, a burst of anger filled her chest. She would not let it end this way, with Rockwell laying blame on the police force while he looked like the hero.

And Jake never knowing how much she loved him.

She might not be strong enough to overpower Death Eyes, but if she could get him to loosen his grip…

With a guttural cry she delivered the palm-heel strike like a pro. He fell to his knees, and she pushed her way through the crowd.

The press continued to fire off questions at the chief, but all Robin could think about was Detective Dunn standing behind Jake. If he didn't get the nod from Death Eyes, he wouldn't stick Jake with the drug, right?

Weaving through the swarm of spectators toward Rockwell, she shouted, "No! Stop! It's Candidate Rockwell." But she was drowned out by the buzz of press questions. She grabbed a nearby reporter. "Rockwell is behind all this."

Death Eyes grabbed her. "Come on, honey, we need to get you back to the hospital."

"Robin!" Jake cried, pushing through the crowd.

"Hey, wait a minute," the reporter protested.

Death Eyes shoved him aside and dragged Robin away.

Suddenly Jake was there, grabbing Death Eyes from behind and yanking him off her. Robin fell to the ground, and the reporter kneeled beside her. They watched Jake and Death Eyes exchange blows.

Uniformed police offers rushed into the crowd and broke it up, cuffing both Jake and Death Eyes.

"No, Jake's innocent!" Robin said.

And that's when she saw Detective Dunn approach Jake and jab him with something.

"No!" Robin launched herself at Dunn and they both went down.

In the blur of commotion, all Robin could think about was saving Jake. Had she gotten to him in time? She couldn't see through the bodies that surrounded her, couldn't see Jake.

"Robin?" a man said, crouching beside her. "I'm Alex."

"I saw Rockwell's assistant at the shooting," Robin said. "He's involved. They're smuggling drugs—"

"Ma'am, you'll have to come with me," a uniformed officer said.

"Don't say anything, Robin," Alex offered. "I'm her attorney," he said to the cop.

"Detective Dunn is bad," she said to Alex as the cop led her away. "He stabbed Jake with the drug and—" She searched the crowd. "Jake! Is Jake okay?"

"Go with the officer, and I'll find out," Alex called back.

The cop led her through the crowd where the police chief waited. "Take her inside," the chief said.

Robin glanced over her shoulder frantically searching for Jake…

And spotted him, unconscious on the ground.

The sound of laughter made Robin jerk awake. It took a second to figure out where she was. The hospital.

She glanced at Jake, lying motionless in the hospital bed, and it all came rushing back: Jenn's betrayal, the press conference and the interrogation that followed.

Between the documentation Detective Beck had recovered from Detective Edwards and Robin's account of the night of the shooting, the police were able to draw a line from the drug-smuggling organization directly to Candidate Rockwell.

Smoke and mirrors, that's what Alex had called it—a nearly perfect plan to draw attention away from Rockwell's illegal business by creating fake police corruption.

Well, it wasn't totally fake. Detective Dunn was a dirty cop who'd dated Jenn, betrayed his fellow officers and drugged Ethan and Jake.

Jenn. Robin sighed, still struggling to understand that betrayal. It was Jenn's key card they'd used to get into the building to lure Detective Edwards to his death. Jenn had been involved from the beginning, which meant Robin's relationship with her wasn't real.

She glanced at Jake. His condition was real, as was her love for him.

"How's he doing?" Detective Beck said, coming into the room on crutches.

"Should you be out of bed, Detective Beck?" she asked.

"Call me Ethan, and, if I stayed in bed one more minute, I might lose it and shoot something." He caught himself. "Sorry, it's just an expression."

"It's okay." She leaned forward and took Jake's hand. "His vitals are good, but until they determine the drug's components, they aren't sure how to treat him, other than let him sleep it off."

Ethan leaned against the wall. "He's tough. He'll be okay."

"He'd better be. All he did was be a Good Samaritan."

"You'd better not be blaming yourself for this."

"Trying not to. Some days I succeed." She glanced at him. "Some days I fail."

He nodded and they shared a moment of concerned silence. "My brother tells me the case is wrapped up. Rockwell is out of politics for good and is facing federal drug charges, his minions are behind bars and Detective Dunn… Well, turns out he was the one who exposed the safe house."

"I still can't believe Jenn was involved."

"It turns out she had some serious financial issues. They paid her for the use of her key card, and one of their guys disabled the lock to the Remmington Imports office so they could cast suspicion on Remmington. She didn't know they planned to kill Officer Edwards."

"She delivered me to Death Eyes," Robin snapped.

"By then, she was in too deep. They were threatening to kill her younger sister if she didn't follow through."

"What about Detective Edwards?" Robin asked.

"My guess is he didn't know who to trust and launched his own investigation."

"Brave man."

"Yeah, kind of like slugger here. I heard Jake did quite a number on the killer's face at city hall."

"You heard right."

"And you? Tackling a dirty cop?" He smiled. "How come I miss all the fun?"

"Ha-ha."

"The department might have more questions for you."

"They know where to find me."

"It could be a while before he wakes up."

If he wakes up.

She didn't answer, emotion clogging her throat.

She took a deep breath. "Why did Rockwell do it?"

"Arrogance, power, money. Take your pick."

"But to go after the Seattle P.D. like that?"

"Like I said, arrogant. He had one cop in his pocket and figured he could use that to sully the whole department."

"And I just happened to be in the wrong place at the wrong time."

"Maybe."

She glanced at Ethan.

"You and Jake never would have met if you hadn't been at work that night. I know he cares about you. A lot."

"Yeah, well." She eyed Jake. "That's a transference thing."

"Is it?"

It had to be. If the past few days had taught her anything it was that she truly couldn't handle this again, handle loving someone so deeply and losing them to a random event of life.

"I'd better get back," Ethan said.

"Thanks for coming by."

"Thanks for being here."

Of course, she'd be here. She'd do whatever she could to help

Jake, whether it was praying at his bedside, talking to him or adjusting his blanket. She'd see this through to the end.

Then she'd leave. She had no choice.

She leaned forward, gripping his hands. "Please come back to us, Jake. Please wake up. I love you."

I love you.

Jake opened his eyes, drifting out of unconsciousness, and thought he saw Robin's beautiful, brown eyes looking down at him.

But the moment flashed too quickly as doctors and nurses hovered around his bed, asking questions, taking vitals and shining a penlight in his eyes.

He wanted to say he was fine, just tired, and he wanted to see Robin, make sure she was okay.

Had he dreamt Robin confessing her love for him?

The whole scene felt surreal. A doctor fired off questions: What's your name? Where are you? What year is it?

He answered the best he could but wanted them gone. The doctor explained he'd been unconscious due to a drug reaction, but his vitals were good, and he'd be fine.

But was Robin fine?

"Where's Robin?" he asked the doctor.

"Who's that? Your wife?" the doctor answered.

Jake wished.

"No, not my wife." But he didn't know what to call her. They hadn't even dated.

"Hey, buddy," Ethan said, passing the doctor as the doctor left the room. "Good to see you with your eyes open."

"You, too. I was out for a few days, huh?"

"Yep. Could have been worse if Robin hadn't shoved Dunn out of the way."

"Dunn?"

"He nailed you with the synthetic drug they used to spike my coffee." Ethan settled in a chair. "You didn't get a lethal dose because Robin tackled the guy."

"You're kidding."

"Nope."

"Where is she?"

Ethan glanced at the floor.

"E, what is it?" Jake pressed.

"She left when you woke up."

"So, she was here?"

"The entire time. Never left your side."

He hadn't dreamt it. She did say the words.

I love you.

"Why did she leave?" Jake asked.

"Keeping vigil by your bed took a lot out of her. I think she blames herself for your condition."

"What!" Jake gripped his head, trying to quell the ache. "That's ridiculous."

"I know that, and you know that, but that pretty thing is blaming herself. The professional in me says guilt might have kept her by your bedside, or maybe transference, but personally I suspect otherwise." He pinned Jake with serious blue eyes. "Don't let her get away, Jake. I can tell she really cares about you and we both know how you feel."

"It's that obvious?"

Ethan smiled. "So, I guess you want to be brought up to speed on the case?"

"Yeah, that would be great."

As Ethan told the story about how Candidate Rockwell was the puppet master behind the scenes, and who was arrested and why, Jake couldn't get the sound of Robin's voice out of his mind.

She loved him but she was gone. Why?

Keeping vigil by your bed took a lot out of her.

Ethan's words coupled with Robin's disappearing act suddenly made sense. Sitting here, praying for him to wake up, had to have reminded her of losing her brother. He knew she kept people at arm's length to protect herself so she'd never have to feel that kind of pain again.

The pain of loss.

Well, Jake was going to take Ethan's advice and not let her get away. He just had to figure out how to approach her without scaring her off.

"Am I boring you?" Ethan smiled.

"Sorry. I drifted."

"I'll bet."

"Hey, you're awake," Robin said coming into the room. "Sorry, I was grabbing a cup of coffee."

Jake felt a rush of awareness and something else. Love.

"He's been asking about you." Ethan stood. "I've got to... Well, I have stuff to do."

Ethan hobbled out of the room, and Robin stood beside Jake's bed.

"I hear you'd make a great linebacker," Jake said.

Robin smiled slightly. "Yeah, well, it was a crazy day." She pinned him with sweet, brown eyes. "I'm so glad you're okay."

"I know."

"You do?"

"I heard you, Robin."

"Oh." She glanced down at her interlaced fingers.

"So, should we schedule a first date?"

She wrapped her arms around her middle. He knew this stance. He didn't like it.

"Robin?"

She snapped her gaze to meet his. "I can't."

"Why not?"

"I made a promise when I was under the truck on the ferry. I promised God that if He saved your life I'd... Well, I'd walk away."

"Robin, God wouldn't want—"

"No. I can't. Okay?" Her eyes welled up.

"Okay. It's okay." But it wasn't. He had no intention of letting her go. "Are you sure that's what this is about?"

"What do you mean?" She studied him.

"I think you're afraid to love again because of the pain you've attached to it."

"I made a promise, Jake, and you're alive and I have to keep my promise," she said, her voice rising in pitch.

"Robin, God is about love, not fear. He wouldn't want you to live without the blessing of love."

"We've known each other less than a week and I was told from the beginning about transference and we both agreed this wasn't a real—"

"Sorry to interrupt, but I need to speak with Jake," the doctor said.

"I was just leaving," Robin said. She shot Jake a sad smile. "Thanks. For everything."

And she left.

EPILOGUE

It was a beautiful day in Seattle, and Robin decided to get out and walk down to The Market. Donuts for lunch would cheer her up. They always did.

Only as she bit into her second one, she realized it had no taste. The vendor had made it the same way, dropped the donut into the bag with powdered sugar and shook it up for her. Everything was the same.

Yet everything was different.

The hole she'd been carrying around with her about her brother's death was bigger, more painful today.

It had been two weeks since she'd seen Jake at the hospital.

God is about love, not fear. He wouldn't want you to live without the blessing of love.

Was he right? Was she using her promise to God as an excuse because she was a coward, afraid to face the pain of loss again?

It didn't matter. The rational side of her brain reminded her that people didn't fall in love during a time of crisis. Heightened emotions and adrenaline could easily be misinterpreted as love.

Keep on telling yourself that, girl.

But no matter how many times she did, the truth always surfaced: she was in love with Jake Walters.

She wandered down to the waterfront, hoping to ease her mind by gazing across Elliott Bay. The water usually calmed her, but today the memory of watching the boats float by in Por

Whisper taunted her. No, she had to put it behind her, focus on her career and meeting new people. Yet she'd only push them away, too, right?

Like she had Jake.

She leaned against the wood railing and gazed at the snow-capped Olympic Mountains in the distance. They used to look vibrant before, awe-inspiring.

Today all she could see was gray haze hovering across the peaks.

Out of the corner of her eye, she noticed a man leaning against the railing a few feet away. She glanced to her right....

Jake.

Her breath caught in her throat. He looked as handsome as ever with his sparkling blue-green eyes and warm smile.

"They're better if you eat them right away." He motioned to the bag in her hand and shifted a few inches closer.

"What are you doing here?"

"Enjoying a beautiful afternoon with my favorite girl?" He shrugged. "I've walked away from my share of things, Robin. I can't walk away from this one."

He reached out.

She hesitated. "I'm scared," she admitted.

"Life is scary. That's why it's better to go through it with someone you love."

She took his hand, and he pulled her against his chest. He wrapped his arms around her and held her close.

"I can't believe you found me," she said.

He tipped her chin up and looked into her eyes.

"We found each other, sweetheart."

He kissed her, and all her fears, all her rationalizations, dissolved. It felt like she was waking up from a bad dream, and she'd been asleep for a very long time.

Jake broke the kiss and smiled down at her. "Don't suppose I can talk you out of a donut?"

* * * * *

Dear Reader:

I've always wondered what it would be like to have a do-over,
shelve the past and start with a fresh slate. Would I be the same
person I was before? Or would I be different?

Witness on the Run challenges my heroine to find strength
in herself and seek guidance from God, although she'd turned
away from Him years ago. Due to her temporary memory loss,
Robin is challenged to take a look at her life from a whole new
perspective and find courage she never thought she had.

I believe we are stronger than we think, especially with the
Lord's guidance and love, and we'll rise to conquer any challenge
if it's important enough to us. Robin's lesson of turning away
from fear and heading toward love and God is a critical lesson,
one that helps her find peace.

I hope you enjoy her journey and find your own inner peace
through God's love.

Hope White

QUESTIONS FOR DISCUSSION

1. Robin's family lost their faith when they lost her brother. Have you known someone who lost faith? How did he/she find the way back to God?

2. How can prayer help someone process a painful memory?

3. Do you sense Robin felt blame for her brother's death? Why or why not?

4. Do you think Robin should have spoken with her parents about her feelings regarding her brother's death? Why or why not?

5. Is keeping people at a distance an effective way to avoid emotional pain?

6. What life lessons did you learn from reading Jake and Robin's story?

7. What did you think was the underlying theme of the book?

8. Who were your favorite secondary characters? Why?

9. Was Jake right in wanting to keep Robin at a distance to protect her? Why or why not?

10. How did Jake open Robin's heart to the Lord?

11. Did you enjoy the history between Jake, Ethan and Morgan? Why?

12. Which character resonated with you the most and why?

INSPIRATIONAL

Inspirational romances to warm your heart & soul.

Love Inspired
SUSPENSE

TITLES AVAILABLE NEXT MONTH

Available June 14, 2011

REQUEST YOUR FREE BOOKS!

2 FREE RIVETING INSPIRATIONAL NOVELS
PLUS 2 FREE MYSTERY GIFTS

Love Inspired
SUSPENSE

YES! Please send me 2 FREE Love Inspired® Suspense novels and my 2 FREE mystery gifts (gifts are worth about $10). After receiving them, if I don't wish to receive any more books, I can return the shipping statement marked "cancel". If I don't cancel, I will receive 4 brand-new novels every month and be billed just $4.24 per book in the U.S. or $4.74 per book in Canada. That's a saving of at least 23% off the cover price. It's quite a bargain! Shipping and handling is just 50¢ per book in the U.S. and 75¢ per book in Canada.* I understand that accepting the 2 free books and gifts places me under no obligation to buy anything. I can always return a shipment and cancel at any time. Even if I never buy another book, the two free books and gifts are mine to keep forever.

123/323 IDN FDCT

Name	(PLEASE PRINT)	

Address		Apt. #

City	State/Prov.	Zip/Postal Code

Signature (if under 18, a parent or guardian must sign)

Mail to the **Reader Service:**
IN U.S.A.: P.O. Box 1867, Buffalo, NY 14240-1867
IN CANADA: P.O. Box 609, Fort Erie, Ontario L2A 5X3

Not valid for current subscribers to Love Inspired Suspense books.

**Are you a subscriber to Love Inspired Suspense
and want to receive the larger-print edition?
Call 1-800-873-8635 or visit www.ReaderService.com.**

* Terms and prices subject to change without notice. Prices do not include applicable taxes. Sales tax applicable in N.Y. Canadian residents will be charged applicable taxes. Offer not valid in Quebec. This offer is limited to one order per household. All orders subject to credit approval. Credit or debit balances in a customer's account(s) may be offset by any other outstanding balance owed by or to the customer. Please allow 4 to 6 weeks for delivery. Offer available while quantities last.

Your Privacy—The Reader Service is committed to protecting your privacy. Our Privacy Policy is available online at www.ReaderService.com or upon request from the Reader Service.

We make a portion of our mailing list available to reputable third parties that offer products we believe may interest you. If you prefer that we not exchange your name with third parties, or if you wish to clarify or modify your communication preferences, please visit us at www.ReaderService.com/consumerchoice or write to us at Reader Service Preference Service, P.O. Box 9062, Buffalo, NY 14269. Include your complete name and address.

LISUS11

*With time running out to stop the Lions of Texas
from orchestrating their evil plan, Texas Ranger
Levi McDonall must work with his childhood friend
to solve his captain's murder and thwart the group's
disastrous plot. Read on for a preview of OUT OF TIME
by Shirlee McCoy, the exciting conclusion to the*
TEXAS RANGER JUSTICE *series.*

Silence told its own story, and Susannah Jorgenson listened as she hurried across the bridge that led to the Alamo Chapel. Darkness had fallen hours ago and the air held a hint of rain. The shadows seemed deeper than usual, the darkness just a little blacker. Or maybe it was simply her imagination that made the Alamo complex seem so forbidding.

She shivered. Not from the cold. Not from the chilly breeze. From the darkness, the silence, the endless echo of her fear as she made her final rounds. She jogged to the chapel and flashed the beam of her light along the corners of the building.

Nothing.

No movement, no sounds, no reason to think she wasn't alone, but she couldn't shake the feeling that she was being watched. That somewhere beyond the beam of her light, danger waited. She did a full sweep of the chapel and of the office area beyond. Nothing, of course.

She opened the chapel door, stepping straight into a broad, muscular chest. Someone grabbed her upper arms, holding her in place.

She shoved forward into her attacker, pushing her weight into a solid wall of strength as she tried to unbalance him.

"Calm down. I was just trying to keep you from falling." The man released his hold.

"Sorry about that. I wasn't expecting anyone to be standing near the door. We're closed for the day, but we'll be open again at seven tomorrow morning." She cleared her throat.

"No need to apologize. I'm Ranger Levi McDonall. My captain said he was going to call and let you know I was on the way."

"Levi McDonall?" Her childhood idol? Her best guy friend? Her first teenage crush?

No way could they be the same.

"Come on in." She hurried into the chapel, trying to pull herself together. This was the Texas Ranger she'd be working with for the next eight days?

She flipped on a light, turned to face McDonall.

Levi McDonall.

Her Levi McDonall.

Can Levi and Susannah put the past behind them to save San Antonio's future? Find out in OUT OF TIME by Shirlee McCoy from Love Inspired Suspense, available in June wherever books are sold.

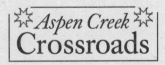
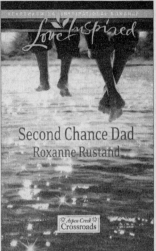